THE LIBERIAN AGENDA

L.J. TAYLOR

Waterview Publishing, LLC

GET A FREE BOOK

Sign up at www.ljtaylorbooks.com/monrovian and get a free copy of one of my books and first dibs on any promotions, appearances and prize giveaways.

Chapter I

His father always kept him waiting. Joseph Saytumah pulled back the sleeve of his custom-made suit jacket, glanced at his watch, and sighed. He'd arrived at the glitzy hotel suite at the Ritz Carlton nearly an hour ago only to be greeted by one of his father's minions and told that the man himself was on a conference call with the president of Liberia.

The door to one of the bedrooms opened. Dwe Saytumah stepped into the living room, his powerful presence immediately filling it.

Joseph, a tall, dark-skinned man with broad shoulders, studied him, looking for any signs of illness. They looked a lot alike -- even had the same build -- but the older man's hair was speckled with grey, while Joseph's was still jet-black. His father was a little thinner than usual, his high cheekbones prominent.

"Joseph." Dwe smiled and threw his arms wide. His deep rich baritone boomed throughout the suite.

"Father." Joseph rose from his seat and stepped forward to embrace him.

"It is good to see you, my son." Dwe stepped back and looked Joseph over. "You look well."

"I am well, Father. How are you? Saye tells me that you have been seeing the family doctor more often lately. Should I be worried?"

Dwe waved a hand. "Nonsense, I am fit as a fiddle as they say here. It was just a bad cold. There is no need for concern."

Another man stepped into the living room. He was tall like Joseph and Dwe and shared the same high cheekbones, but there the resemblance ended. He was lighter in complexion, with a sharply pointed nose and a goatee.

Joseph felt his shoulders tense. He tried to shake off the tension as he prepared to greet his brother. As children, they had been very close – inseparable even. Joseph had looked up to Saye, seeing him as his hero and protector until one day it became abundantly clear that Saye couldn't protect him. Their relationship changed forever that day, and, as the years passed, the chasm between them had widened. The last time he saw Saye, his brother's bitterness had threatened to spill over.

This time, Joseph was better prepared. He'd made arrangements to keep Saye happy. He plastered a smile on his face and crossed the room. "Brother." He put his arms around Saye and gave him a hug.

Saye pounded him on the back. "Hey there, baby brother. I see that America is treating you well."

Joseph chuckled. "It is nothing compared to the royal treatment you and Father receive back home."

Dwe's bodyguard poured them drinks and they settled down in the living room to talk.

"It has been far too long since we last saw you," Dwe said. "It is difficult sometimes having you so far away, but I know that you do it for the good of the family."

Saye twisted his lips. "What do you mean? He does it for the good of himself. Who wouldn't want to live in New York with the great nightlife and the women of easy virtue? I can't wait to get out there. How long are we going to be cooped up in here?"

Dwe frowned at Saye. "For as long as it takes. It would do you good to remember that we are here for business and not pleasure. Of course, pleasure is all you can think about. If you ever wondered why I sent Joseph here to school instead of you, it is because I feared you would get so caught up in this hedonistic lifestyle that you would never finish."

"But Father, I am the eldest. It is my birthright to take the reins of the business and represent our family here in the States," Saye said.

"With a birthright comes responsibility, Saye. That is something you have never shown me you were willing to take on. Your brother, on the other hand, showed both the willingness and the ability to take the reins from an early age."

Saye scowled. "I am so sick of hearing about how Joseph is the better son. He has always been your favorite."

Joseph raised his hands in front of him, palms facing outward. "Please. Let us not ruin your visit by fighting. Let us deal with the task at hand so that Saye can enjoy the rest of his time here in New York."

Dwe continued to frown at Saye staring him down until the younger man squirmed and lowered his gaze. Only then did he turn to Joseph. "The authorities are beginning to watch the diplomatic pouches more closely."

"That's true," Saye said. "The orders are getting bigger and the embassy is starting to ask questions. I don't know how much longer we can hold them off. Why don't we just transport the shipments on our jet or hire a company to handle that for us?"

"Not with the heightened restrictions put on air travel since September 11," Joseph said. "Besides, who would we trust to transport our merchandise? A better idea would be to acquire a controlling interest in a shipping company. There are always inspectors at the ports who, for the right price, are willing to look the other way. I read in the paper that a well-known American shipping line is in financial trouble and in desperate need of a white knight. Perhaps we should come to their rescue."

Dwe nodded. "That sounds like a good idea, son. We will need an American attorney to represent us in the transaction. Someone established with a powerful law firm to back them. You know the American government will be suspicious when it learns that a Liberian company is seeking to buy an American shipping line."

"I have just the right person in mind," Joseph said.

"Who would that be?" Dwe asked.

"Do you remember my friend Sonia?"

"Do you mean that sexy bitch who wanted nothing to do with you after a few short months? What can she do?" Saye asked.

"Careful brother," Joseph said. "She may end up being my wife."

"You were always obsessed with her. I never understood it. Why her over all the beautiful women in the world?" Saye asked.

"You don't understand. She is now a partner at a prominent law firm here in New York. She negotiates deals like this for a living and, with her connections, she should be able to get us the introductions we need," Joseph said.

Dwe stood. "Contact her then and set up a meeting. Now, if you don't mind, my sons, it has been a long journey. I require rest."

Joseph rose and nodded. "Of course, Father. I will come see you tomorrow."

The two brothers watched their father retire to his bedroom. Saye then grinned and rubbed his hands together. "Now that business is over, little brother, show me where the women are."

Joseph's smile was indulgent. "With pleasure. I have made arrangements for you to be taken to the hottest nightclubs in the City tonight -- V.I.P. access. The car will come for you at ten o'clock. Have a good time."

Saye's eyes lit up like a kid in a candy store. Grinning from ear to ear, he clapped Joseph hard on the shoulder with a large beefy hand. Joseph winced.

"Now that's what I'm talking about little brother," he said. A puzzled frown appeared on his brow a second later. "Wait a minute. You're not coming with me?"

Joseph shook his head. "Not my thing. You know that. Besides, I have to make arrangements to hire Sonia."

"You are going to a lot of trouble to secure one piece of ass," Saye said.

"She is much more than that, my brother. So much more," Joseph said. "Have a great time tonight. You can tell me all about it tomorrow."

"I will," Saye promised.

***

Sonia sat in her office reviewing an agreement virtually covered in red ink. She shook her head. *What a mess*, she thought. *It would have been easier to just draft the damned thing myself.*

The telephone rang. Red pen poised, she turned to look at the caller I.D. display. It was the managing partner's assistant, Gina.

Sonia groaned. Whenever Gina called her, it was usually not to impart good news. The last time had been to schedule a meeting with Gordon wherein he had lectured her for twenty minutes about how she needed to get out from behind her desk and network more so she could meet people and bring in business.

Easy for him to say. She wasn't an extrovert like Gordon. She hated attending social functions and avoided them like the plague. Being the daughter of a United States Senator meant being forced to attend an endless number of boring functions. Once she'd escaped from her parents' home, she'd vowed never to find herself in that position again. Ironically, her choice of profession required her to network.

Sighing, she snatched up the telephone handset and put it to her ear. "This is Sonia."

"Sonia! It's Gina. Gordon wants to see you right away."

"Right now? What about?"

"It probably has something to do with that tall, dark and oh so handsome new client I just escorted into his office," Gina said.

Sonia smiled. Maybe Gina was giving her good news after all. "Well, in that case, maybe I should get up there right away."

"Oh you definitely should, girlie," Gina said.

Sonia chuckled. "On my way."

She arrived at Gordon's office moments later and knocked on the door.

"Come in," Gordon said.

Sonia walked into the large, plush, modern office. Gordon sat behind his desk and the client who, from what Sonia could see, was a dark-skinned Black man in a light gray suit, sat in one of the guest chairs. He didn't turn to look at her so she couldn't see his face but there was something vaguely familiar about him.

Gordon looked up at her. "Sonia, I've just been getting acquainted with an old friend of yours who's about to become our newest client -- Joseph Saytumah." He gestured toward the client who now stood up and turned to face her.

Sonia felt her jaw go slack and her eyes widen. Her mind went completely blank for a moment. *Joseph?* Talk about a blast from the past. She'd thought she'd never see him again. *What was he doing here?* And what did Gordon mean by "our newest client?" Realizing how visibly shocked she looked, she snapped her mouth shut and made an effort to regain her composure.

Joseph smiled at her. She walked over to him. "Joseph? Oh my God. How long has it been?" She held out a hand for a handshake.

Joseph clasped it warmly in both of his. "Sonia. You are as lovely as ever." He released her hand, took her by the shoulders and kissed her soundly on both cheeks, European-style. Sonia glanced over at Gordon, who watched then, looking amused. She felt the heat rise in her face. Not knowing quite how to react, she patted Joseph awkwardly on the shoulders with both hands. When he finally released her, she quickly took a step back.

"Thank you," she said. "Please, have a seat."

She gestured toward the chair he had abandoned. Maybe if he sat down, he wouldn't be tempted to grab her again. She stifled a sigh of relief when he took his seat. She took the other visitor's chair. "So, Joseph, what brings you here?"

"His company is doing a business deal and he wants to hire us, and more specifically you, to represent them in the transaction," Gordon said.

"I remembered that you went to a great law school and I heard that you had become a partner here. So when my father said we needed a lawyer to represent us in this deal, I knew you would be perfect for the job," Joseph said.

Sonia felt a slight chill dance down her spine. He'd heard that she made partner at the law firm? She wondered where he'd heard that and how he even knew where she worked. Did he really just hear it through the grapevine or had he kept tabs on her all these years? She remembered how he'd called her up out of the blue one evening in Philly when she'd gone to a lot of trouble to keep him from finding out which law school she'd planned to attend. He'd hired a private investigator to track her down even though they'd broken up months before.

She was tempted to ask him how he had found her, but noticed Gordon staring at her and decided to hold her tongue. He inclined his head slightly, as if willing her to respond to Joseph's comment. He was probably wondering what the hell was wrong with her.

She cleared her throat. "Oh, really? Well, I'm flattered. What business are you in again?"

"Import/export," he said.

"Oh yes, that's right. And what type of deal did you want us to assist you with?" she asked.

"We want to acquire the assets of an American shipping company," he said.

"That's right up your alley, Sonia. You negotiate deals like this all the time," Gordon said.

"Yes. That's true," she said.

Whereas normally during a pitch to a prospective client, she would have touted her experience, Sonia decided to remain quiet. Import/export? Well it didn't get vaguer than that. She'd had her suspicions about Joseph's family business since college. He was always travelling on "business" trips back then and he was always very mysterious when she had asked about them.

Although he was just a college student back then, he drove a late model luxury sedan and was very generous -- buying her expensive gifts, taking her to the nicest restaurants, and getting front row seats at music concerts. Despite the perks, the evasive manner in which he answered her questions about his business trips had caused her to believe the family business might not be legit. At one point she'd even imagined they were drug traffickers. She couldn't let his company become a client of the law firm until she checked them out. Thoroughly. The last thing she needed was to cause the firm problems by bringing in a shady client. She looked up to find Gordon staring at her again.

"Well," Gordon said, "I'm sure you two old friends want to get reacquainted. Sonia, why don't you take Mr. Saytumah out for a drink? We can take care of the formalities of the retainer agreement tomorrow."

Joseph smiled. "That sounds like an excellent idea."

It was a terrible idea. She needed to process all this and figure out her next step before sitting down with Joseph one-on-one. She tried to beg off. "Oh, but I have this agreement I need to work on tonight."

"Nonsense." Gordon waved his hand dismissively. "Give the agreement to Sally or work on it tomorrow." He stood up, walked around his desk, and shook Joseph's hand. "It was a pleasure to meet you, Joseph. Thank you for agreeing to retain our firm for your deal. You're in excellent hands now."

"The very best I am sure," Joseph said. "I look forward to having a mutually beneficial working relationship with this law firm." With that, he headed toward the door and stepped out of Gordon's office into the hallway.

Sonia turned to follow him, but Gordon stopped her. "Sonia, what's wrong with you? Don't cross-examine him. Be nice to him."

"Of course. Sorry if I acted strangely. I was just a little shocked to see him sitting here. I haven't seen him since college," she said.

Gordon studied her for a moment, then nodded. "All right, then. Go bring home the bacon."

"Yes sir," she said.

She walked out of Gordon's office wondering how she was going to handle the situation. There was no way to avoid going out for drinks with Joseph. Gordon would pimp her out to the devil himself if it meant bringing in business for the law firm. She would just have to start her research into Joseph and his company a little later.

***

Sonia decided to take Joseph to an upscale bar in Midtown not far from the office. She often went there with some of her colleagues for happy hour. On Fridays, the place was a "meet market" -- standing room only and filled with predators looking for easy prey. Because it was a weeknight, the bar was half-empty and they had their choice of seating arrangements. She chose a cocktail table in a quiet corner of the bar. They ordered drinks and engaged in small talk until the waitress delivered them.

Sonia took a sip of her Cosmopolitan and decided to ask Joseph the question that had been burning foremost in her mind. "So, how did you know that I was at the firm?"

"Well, one day I opened the newspaper and there was a picture of you with an announcement that you had made partner. I thought I would never see you again, and there you were, right here in New York City," he said.

"You live in the City? How long have you been here?" she asked.

"Almost two years now," he said.

Sonia shook her head. She couldn't believe she hadn't run into him in the past two years. The island wasn't that big. On the other hand, she worked so much that she rarely ventured out.

"What brought you here?" she asked.

"I moved here for work. In addition to working for my father's company, I work for the Liberian Consulate here in New York," he said.

"I can't believe that we've both been living in the City and we've never run into each other," she said.

"It is not so surprising to me. I travel a great deal in connection with my work. So, tell me, what have you been doing all these years besides working your way to the top? Are you married yet? Do you have any children?" he asked.

"No. Being a career woman doesn't leave a lot of time for that sort of thing," she said.

"A beautiful woman like you cannot possibly be single. Some man must have snapped you up by now," he said.

"Well, thank you for the compliment," she said. "I date, of course, but I haven't yet met the right man to settle down with. What about you? Are you married?"

"No. I am still waiting for the right woman to take my hand," he said. He looked her in the eye and then slid his hand across the table to cover one of hers.

What the hell?

Did he honestly believe she'd fall for such an obvious move? She needed to nip this in the bud -- especially if they were going to be working together as attorney and client. She pulled her hand out from underneath his, cleared her throat and changed the subject.

"Tell me about your father's business. What exactly do you import and export?" she asked.

Joseph shrugged. "Whatever happens to be profitable at the time. Typically, we export Liberian products and import items that Liberia needs such as vehicles, supplies, electronics, and other finished products."

"I see. So, which company does your father wish to acquire and why?" she asked.

"A small shipping company called Portside Marine. Having a shipping company would provide another stream of revenue and solve some of our transportation issues at the same time. In the import/export business, shipping is one of our biggest expenses next to taxes and tariffs," he said.

"That makes sense," Sonia said. And it did. Maybe, just maybe, Joseph's company was legit.

Please let that be the case.

"Have you ever negotiated this type of deal before?" he asked.

"Yes. In fact, earlier this year I helped a client acquire a shipping company. Are you sure you want to buy the company? It might be more advantageous to just buy the company's assets. We could have one of my tax partners take a look at the deal and figure out the best way to structure it."

"That sounds like a very good idea," he said.

"Good. Well, tomorrow we'll run a conflict check to make sure there's no problem with the firm representing you in this transaction. If there's no conflict, then we'll make arrangements for you to execute a retainer agreement and wire the retainer fee to our account," she said.

"Of course. Just send me the wire transfer instructions and the letter and we will take care of that immediately. My father and brother will want to meet with you to discuss the finer points of the deal," he said.

"Yes. We'll certainly need to have more in-depth discussions about what you're trying to achieve so we can make it happen," she said.

Joseph looked at his watch. "I would ask you to join me for dinner, but I have another engagement tonight."

"I understand. I have to get back to work myself," she said. She needed to get that background check going.

She signaled the waiter for the check. When she reached over to take it, Joseph snatched it out of her hand. She frowned. "Hey! What are you doing? The drinks are on the firm to welcome you as a new client."

"No, my lady," he said, "the drinks are on me."

She shrugged. "Well, if you insist."

Joseph raised his eyebrows. "I see that you have mellowed quite a bit since the old days at Vassar. The old Sonia would have called me a chauvinist pig."

Sonia laughed. "Well, the firm frowns on us calling clients names."

Joseph chuckled. "Yes. That would not be very good for business."

He paid the bill. They gathered their things and headed outside. A black town car pulled up in front of the restaurant.

"This is my car," he said. "Can I give you a ride anywhere?"

"No, thank you. I'm going to catch a cab," she said.

Joseph hailed a taxi. He opened the taxi door for her and she climbed inside. He held the door open for a moment. "I look forward to hearing from you regarding the retainer and setting up the meeting with my family."

"I'll run the conflict check tomorrow. I'll call you if there are any issues. Thank you for the drinks. Take care," she said.

"And you, my lady." He shut the taxi door and took a step back.

Sonia gave her address to the driver and slumped against the back seat. She had a lot to think about.

**

Joseph watched Sonia's taxi drive off. He knew she was not yet fully convinced she should represent his company. She never did trust him or his work. He smiled and shook his head. His Sonia was no fool.

He climbed into the back of the town car. "Take me to the warehouse in Brooklyn."

"Yes sir," the driver said.

He arrived at the warehouse twenty minutes later. His man and Saye were already waiting outside. He got out of the car and walked up to them. "Are they here yet?"

Saye nodded. "Yes. We got here early. They were already inside when we arrived."

"Alright," Joseph said. "Follow me." He turned and walked toward the entrance of the warehouse, the two men following close behind him. He walked through the door and up to the table where the Russians were doing shots of vodka. Two men followed them in aiming machine guns at their backs. Joseph kept walking focusing his attention on Dmitri -- the leader of the pack. He smiled at Dmitri who waived the armed men off with a jerk of his head. They backed off and headed outside to guard the entrance.

"Hello Dmitri," Joseph said.

Dmitri stood and threw his arms wide. "Joseph, my dear friend." He moved forward to embrace him. "How are you? I was happy to receive your call. It has been a while."

Joseph patted him on the back. "Yes it has, old friend."

Dmitri pulled back and took a look at Saye. "I do not believe I've had the pleasure of meeting this gentleman before."

"Dmitri, this is my brother Saye. Saye, this is my friend Dmitri. We are old college buddies," Joseph said.

Saye stepped forward to shake Dmitri's hand. "It is a pleasure to meet you. Any friend of Joseph's is a friend of the family."

Dmitri returned the handshake and then gestured toward the table. "Please, have a seat. We'll have drinks."

Joseph and Saye sat down. Joseph's man, however, remained standing.

One of Dmitri's men brought a new bottle of vodka and clean glasses to the table. Shots were poured and distributed.

Dmitri raised his glass. "To long-legged women and great friends."

"Hear hear." The men raised their glasses, drained them and slammed them down onto the table.

"So, to what do I owe the pleasure?" Dmitri asked.

"This is about what we can do for each other," Joseph said. We are about to enter into a very lucrative shipping arrangement that could result in a mutually satisfying relationship. We need to order a large shipment of weapons from you. In exchange, we can assist you with transporting shipments ordered by your other customers anywhere in the world. We could do that for a cash payment or for credit toward our purchases. That is something we can negotiate."

Dmitri stroked his beard. "Hmmm . . . transportation is always an issue in our business as you know. And it's much better to have it provided by people you trust. What type of weapons are we talking about?"

"We need to equip a small army," Joseph said. "We need everything from machine guns to grenade launchers to explosives and ammunition. Can you handle that?"

Dmitri nodded. "Yes. We can handle that. How soon do you need it?"

"We will have the transportation online in no more than six weeks," Joseph said. "We will be able to take our first shipment at that time."

"That is excellent," Dmitri said. "I have a customer who expects to receive a shipment in the Ivory Coast in eight weeks. We would normally pay three hundred thousand U.S. for transport of that size shipment. We can deduct that from the cost of your order and consider this a trial run."

Joseph was careful not to allow his disappointment to show on his face. He knew that Dmitri normally paid half a million dollars for arms shipments to the Ivory Coast. The bribes alone would take up a good chunk of the proposed fee. He glanced at Saye to make sure he didn't react negatively. At best, a bad reaction could damage the relationship he had been so careful to cultivate with Dmitri. At worst, the volatile Russian could get angry and they'd have to shoot their way out. While that might be Saye's way -- it was not Joseph's. He preferred to fight his battles in a different way -- to use strategy instead of blunt force. Saye's face was impassive. For the moment, he seemed content to let Joseph handle things. He would have to negotiate a very good price on the weapons to make up for some of the loss on the shipping discount.

Joseph smiled at Dmitri. "Excellent. I am sure we can come to a mutually satisfying arrangement on the arms shipment."

Dmitri nodded. "Yes of course, old friend. We always do."

Joseph lifted the vodka bottle and poured Dmitri a shot. He poured one for himself and raised his glass. "I propose a toast. To new beginnings."

Dmitri raised his glass. "To new beginnings, my friend. He knocked his glass against Joseph's.

Chapter II

Tyrone and Tara Nkrumah entered the headquarters of the ATG -- a clandestine unit of the CIA tasked to handle operations pertaining to Africa and the Middle East. Located in Midtown Manhattan, it appeared to be just another high-rise office building. They took one of the elevators up to the thirteenth floor and crossed over to another elevator bank. Tara took out her I.D. card and swiped it over the sensor that took the place of the elevator call button. The doors slid open. She and Tyrone stepped in and rode up to the 27th floor. This time, the doors opened to reveal a woman sitting at a reception desk.

"Hi Rachel," Tyrone said.

"Good afternoon folks," the woman said. "Please step up to the scanner for verification."

Tyrone and Tara stepped up to the ocular scanners and carefully positioned their heads so the machine could scan their eyes. A misread could result in one or more of them being shot. Security was extra-tight these days. After a moment, a tone sounded, and the wall behind the reception desk opened up. They stepped through, walked down a short corridor and entered a hub of activity.

The space was circular and modern and took up two floors. Offices, file rooms, pantries, copy rooms, media rooms, computer rooms, and other useful spaces made up the outer circle of the lower floor. Inside the circle was a large bull pen containing several desks manned by what appeared to be a veritable United Nations. Men and women of all different races, ages, and ethnicities peered into computer screens, typed up reports, talked on telephones, engaged in heated debates, pored over maps or thumbed through paper files.

Tara greeted a very pretty young Asian woman with red highlights streaming through her otherwise jet black hair. "Hey Naimah."

Naimah looked up and smiled. "Tara! Long time no see. How long will you be in New York this time?"

"We'll be here for a few days."

"Good. We should have time to go out for a drink then."

"I'll let you know after we meet with the boss."

Moments later, Tyrone and Tara stepped into their handler's office. Ben Davis, a short wiry man with steel-blue eyes that could pin a suspect or agent to the wall in an instant, peered at them over the metal rims of his glasses.

"So, what have our friends have been up to lately?" he asked.

"The Minister and his oldest son, Saye, met with Joseph Saytumah at their hotel this morning," Tyrone said.

"We know that the Minister has been planning a coup for some time now. The only question is when," Tara said.

"Your job is to stop that coup from happening. As you know, the Minister has anti-American leanings and is likely to align Liberia with other anti-American nations in the region. The current regime is the best hope for that country we've seen in a long, long time. We can't afford to lose that alliance," Ben said.

"Understood. Tara and I have made some progress in infiltrating the Saytumah family's inner social circle. We've established close ties with Joseph Saytumah. The Minister is planning to have a party to celebrate his birthday in a few weeks. With such a large presence in the family compound, we should be able to get into his computer system and find out what we can about his operation and his plans."

"Who are you planning to use?" Ben asked. "I don't want you to break cover."

"I think Jared would be a good candidate for this op," Tara said. "He could pose as our new driver. That would give him access to the mansion. He could make a detour to Dwe's office on the pretext of looking for a restroom." Jared was a new recruit Tara had brought into the fold. He was the first agent she had ever recruited and trained.

Ben nodded. "Yes. That might work. Jared has received excellent reports from his handlers over the past year. You did an excellent job training him."

Tara smiled, her chest filling with pride. She couldn't take all the credit though. Jared was a natural. He'd taken to the training like a duck to water and had excelled in every category.

"Thank you, sir."

Ben nodded again. "Your plan sounds good. Implement it. And keep an eye on the Saytumah family's activities in New York. I want to know who their contacts are and what they're doing at all times."

"Yes sir. That shouldn't be a problem," Tara said. "Saye has a weakness for the ladies and loves to frequent nightclubs. We'll set him up with a couple of dates. Also, we can arrange for Tyrone to run into Joseph while we're here. He knows we travel to the U.S. from time to time to visit relatives. And, of course, we'll have the usual surveillance measures."

"Good," Ben said. "I look forward to receiving your reports. Dismissed."

"Yes sir," Tara and Tyrone said in unison. They left Ben's office.

"Do you really think Jared's ready for this?" Tyrone asked. "I know you trained him and all, and that he's gotten some good reviews, but this is a very dangerous mission. He doesn't have that much experience."

Tara suppressed her immediate instinct to defend Jared and considered Tyrone's words.

Although Jared was her baby brother, she'd learned to trust his instincts over the years they'd worked together. He was a solid agent who should have risen higher in the ranks than he had. He just had no stomach for agency politics – a fact that sometimes landed him in hot water.

"I think he's ready." Tara said. "And Ben agrees with me. Is there something specific I should know about him?"

Tyrone shook his head. "No. I just thought I'd raise the issue given the fact that the kid is fresh out of training."

Tara smiled and patted Tyrone's arm. "Don't worry, little brother, the kid's not about to take your place."

Tyrone grinned. "I'm so glad you put me at ease on that score. I was so afraid of that."

Tara laughed. "Let's go. We need to put this mission together."

***

Sonia stepped into her apartment, locked the door behind her, and began stripping as she walked down the narrow hallway to her bedroom. She hung up her suit, threw her blouse into the hamper and pulled on a tee shirt and a pair of old sweatpants.

She headed into the kitchen and poured herself a glass of wine. She took it into the living room, plopped down on the couch, and tried to make sense of the day. But all she could think about was how handsome Joseph looked and the scent of his cologne. She shook her head. She needed to talk to someone about this. She picked up the telephone and dialed her best friend's number. Charlene picked up on the third ring.

"Hello." She sounded a little breathless.

Sonia raised her eyebrows. "I hope I'm not interrupting anything."

"No, silly. I just walked in. What's up?"

"Girl, you will never guess who I ran into today," Sonia said.

"Who?"

"Joseph Saytumah."

"What? You mean that African guy you dated back in college? No."

"Yes. He walked into my firm, met with the head partner and told him he wanted to hire me to negotiate a deal for his father's company."

"How did he look?"

Sonia laughed. "As fine as ever. But is that all you can think about, Charlene? I really have a problem here."

"Yeah, deciding whether or not to let that brother back into the sheets. Didn't he rock your world back then?" Charlene asked.

"Yeah, but he was also ridiculously jealous and possessive. I had to let him go," Sonia said.

"Just the way I like them -- tall, dark, built and possessive," Charlene said.

Sonia snorted. "Charlene!" She shook her head. What had made her think that Charlene -- whose hormones were always on overdrive -- could help her make sense of this?

"On a more serious note though, what type of business is he in? If memory serves me right, you always suspected he was into something illegal, like drugs. Of course, you always did have a wild imagination," Charlene said.

"And now you see my problem. I always believed he was into something illegal because he was always so mysterious about the family business. He was always taking these trips but I never got a straight answer out of him when I asked what the business entailed and what part he played in it," Sonia said.

"Well, when you saw him today, did you ask him?" Charlene asked.

"Of course I did. He told me they were in the import/export business. He told me the same thing back then. I just didn't believe him. If I bring them in as clients and they turn out to be into something illegal that would not bode well for my career or the law firm. On the other hand, Gordon wants me to start bringing in business so badly, he practically pimped me out this afternoon. He sent us out to "catch up" over drinks and ordered me to be nice to Joseph. What should I do?"

"Well, under the circumstances, there's not much you can do but check them out and keep your eyes open. If you find out something concrete, you can bring it to Gordon's attention. Otherwise, this might be a lucky break for you," Charlene said.

"Yeah, but how am I going to handle Joseph? I mean, he asked me if I was married, he paid me all these compliments, and he looked at me as if I were lunch and he was starving." Sonia said.

Charlene laughed. "Is he married?"

"No, but that's not the point. Do you remember how obsessed he became in college? I can't risk something like that happening again and causing me problems at the firm," Sonia said.

"Well, I would just make it clear that this is strictly a business relationship and nothing more. He's an old friend who brought you a bit of business. That's all," Charlene said.

Sonia shook her head. "I don't know if I can pull that off. We've always had such strong reactions to each other."

"That's true. I remember you used to come back from a night out with him with a smile on your face and a glazed look in your eye," Charlene said.

Sonia laughed. "We certainly did enjoy each other. I remember one time he was mad at me for cursing him out . . ."

As she told the story, it was 1989 again, her last year in college. Joseph had acted like a jealous maniac, calling her at six in the morning and demanding to know where she'd been the night before. Unfortunately for him, she'd been working half the night on her senior thesis and wasn't a morning person. Instead of answering his question, she'd told him off and then hung up on him.

He called her back that afternoon to ask her out to dinner. Feeling a little guilty about the way she'd treated him, she accepted.

He picked her up promptly at 7:00 p.m. He didn't say much when he greeted her. He just gave her a polite peck on the cheek, helped her into the car and got behind the wheel without saying another word. They exited the campus through the main gate and headed toward a nearby diner. The silence between them became unbearable.

She turned to look at him. His gaze was focused on the road, his expression inscrutable. "About this morning. I'm sorry. I was stressed out and tired. I didn't mean to go off on you like that. I'm not used to having to answer to anybody concerning my whereabouts so when you demanded to know where I'd been, I went ballistic. I realize now that I could have called you. I was just trying to get my thesis done."

"Do not worry, my lady. I understand that you American women are very independent and not used to us Liberian men. You will have the opportunity to pay for the things you said this morning." He flashed a wolfish grin at her then reached over and slowly ran his hand up her leg and under her skirt. His fingers trailed the sensitive skin of her inner thigh from her knee to her groin. Sonia gasped and squirmed. What he was doing felt good. He smiled and removed his hand.

He took her to the diner. They chatted about her thesis, his classes, and other things. Sonia was distracted throughout the entire meal thinking about what was to come. Her appetite suffered.

Joseph teased her. "I thought you were hungry, my dear. We should have the waitress wrap your food up and take it to go. You will definitely have an appetite later."

Sonia hit him on the arm. Little butterflies danced in her stomach. They hadn't been dating long and had only had sex a couple of times. Her face warmed as she thought about those encounters. Joseph was a skilled and demanding lover. She didn't know what he had in mind for her. She just hoped to survive it. The last time they made love, he almost drove her crazy. She never knew she could have multiple orgasms.

They left the restaurant soon thereafter. He didn't take the road leading back to the campus.

"Where are you taking me?" Sonia asked.

"To the house where we may enjoy some privacy," he said.

There wasn't enough privacy at the dorm? What did he plan to do to her?

He pulled into his driveway and shut the car off. He then turned to her, grabbed her by the shoulders, jerked her toward him and kissed her roughly. She was lightheaded and breathless when he broke off the kiss.

He helped her out of the car and led her by the hand to his front door. He opened it, drew her inside, closed it, and rammed her back against it with his body. He ravaged her lips. She moaned. He pulled away and looked at her. She sagged against the door, looking back at him.

"It is now time to pay for your earlier behavior, my lady," he said.

"Oh yeah? What do you have in mind?" she asked.

Joseph took her by the hand and led her into the living room. He brought her to stand a few feet in front of the couch and released her. He sat down on the couch facing her.

"Take off your clothes," he said.

Sonia giggled. "Right here?"

"Yes. Do it," he said.

"Yes sir." She kicked off her sandals and reached down to pull her shirt slowly over her head. Next, she unbuttoned her skirt, pulled it over her hips and let it drop to the floor. She stepped out of it and kicked it aside. She then put her hands on her hips and posed a little in her bra and panties. "Now what?"

Joseph took his time and looked her over slowly. He licked his full lips. "Take it all off."

Sonia hooked her hands into her bra straps and peeled her bra down over her shoulders. Turning it around, she unhooked it and threw it aside. Next, she slid her fingers into the elastic waistband of her panties, peeled them over her hips and pushed them down her legs. She stood there completely naked and looked at him.

Joseph stared at her for a moment, drinking in every inch of her body. Then he looked up into her eyes. The hunger she saw there made her shiver. "Come here."

Sonia walked slowly toward him until she was standing between his legs with her shins up against the couch.

He leaned forward, kissed her belly and ran his hands up and down the backs of her legs and over her behind. He grabbed her buttocks with one hand and pushed her pelvis forward. Sonia moaned when the fingers of his other hand slid across and then into the folds of her vagina and found her clitoris. He held her in place while he worked her with his fingers. It felt so good. She moaned and writhed against his fingers.

He let go of Sonia's buttocks and brought his hand back against them sharply. The sting and the shock made Sonia yelp and jerk her pelvis forward against his fingers. She moaned. He repeated the process, spanking and pleasuring her at the same time until her senses overloaded and she could no longer differentiate between the pleasure and the pain. She came so hard that her legs almost collapsed beneath her.

Joseph rose from the couch, got behind her and pushed her forward. She landed on her knees on the edge of the couch, her hands resting against its back. She heard him unbuckle his belt and the sound of his pants hitting the floor. He yanked her hips back and pressed down between her shoulders until she was bent over, her behind high in the air. He spread her legs wide, positioned himself at her entrance and rammed himself into her in a single stroke.

His well-endowed member stretched her wide. Pain and pleasure caused her to cry out as he plunged in and out of her, his hand grasping her hips and yanking her back onto him again and again. After a while, the pain disappeared, leaving only pleasure. He rode her long and hard until she had two more orgasms.

"Damn that sounds good right about now," Charlene said, bringing Sonia back to the present.

"It does, doesn't it? Oh, what am I going to do Charlene? With memories like these, it's going to be hard to keep our relationship strictly professional," Sonia said.

"Hell, with memories like that, I might have to jump him," Charlene said.

"Charlene!"

"Just kidding. Sort of. Look, there's no use agonizing over it. It sounds to me like your managing partner isn't giving you much of a choice. Just handle the transaction, keep your eyes open, and take it one step at a time. A lot of things can change in thirteen years."

"You're probably right. What would I do without you?" Sonia asked.

"I don't know -- trip down memory lane with somebody else?"

Sonia laughed.

***

The next day, Tara and Tyrone met with Jared and told him about the mission.

He could barely contain his excitement. "You mean I finally get to work with you two? The baddest spooks in the agency?"

Tyrone threw him a sharp glance. "I suggest you pay close attention to what we're about to tell you. This is a very dangerous mission. Liberia is no joke. If they catch you, that's your ass. The last thing I need is for some fool to blow our cover and get us all killed."

Jared sucked his teeth. "Can't a brother celebrate for a split second?"

Tyrone and Tara simply stared at him. He sobered, settled back into his chair, and crossed his arms. "Please proceed."

"Thank you," Tara said. "You're going to pose as our driver." She picked up a laser pointer and aimed it at a schematic on a large screen that took up the far wall. "This is the front entrance to the mansion and the driveway." She outlined the area on the screen. "The drivers are usually allowed into the kitchen to get snacks and into this foyer to wait for their employers. They're also allowed to use this guest restroom in the servants' quarters over here. It just so happens that Dwe Saytumah's study is in the same wing of the house as the servants' quarters. It's down this corridor which is near the guest bathroom. The night of the party is the first time you'll visit the Saytumah mansion. You'll establish yourself as our new driver and then get lost on your way to the restroom."

Jared nodded. "Understood."

"The Saytumah mansion has a state-of-the-art security system in addition to the armed security guards patrolling the grounds. That's why the mission must be completed by someone already on the inside," Tara said.

Tyrone chimed in. "From what we can tell, Dwe keeps his information on a stand-alone system in his office. Since it's not hooked up to the Internet, we have no way of hacking into it remotely. We have to set up a link and upload it from the inside." He held out what appeared to be a simple U.S.B. flash drive. "Once you get inside the study, turn on the computer and plug this baby in. The device will do the rest."

"How long will I need to be in there?" Jared asked.

Tyrone shrugged. "It depends on how much data is on the hard drive. Not more than five minutes or so. Naimah will let you know when the upload is complete. We'll be monitoring your progress; however, we're under orders not to blow our cover under any circumstances. Do you understand? If you get caught, you're on your own."

Jared nodded. "Understood."

"I have every faith in you," Tara said. "I know how good you are. After all, I trained you myself."

Jared smiled. "Why thank you, sensei." He steepled his hands together under his chin and bowed his head in mock deference.

Tara laughed and returned the bow. "Make me proud, grasshopper."

Tyrone shook his head at their antics.

***

Sonia's assistant Suzette led Joseph, Saye and Dwe Saytumah into the conference room where Sonia waited. "Gentlemen, this is my boss, Sonia Johnson. I'm leaving you in good hands. Sonia will call me to escort you out when you're ready to leave. It has been a pleasure to meet you."

"No, the pleasure has been all ours to meet such a beautiful and gracious lady," Saye said.

Suzette smiled, clearly enjoying the attention.

Sonia cleared her throat. "Thank you, Suzette."

Suzette nodded and left the room.

Sonia approached the men. Before she could say anything, Joseph grabbed her by the shoulders, pulled her in and kissed her on both cheeks. "Sonia, I would like to introduce you to my father, Dwe Saytumah, and my brother, Saye."

Sonia extended her hand to Dwe first. Instead of shaking it, however, he clasped it between two of his and held it. It was a little awkward, but there was a twinkle in the old man's eye and she didn't have the heart to snatch her hand back. As a senator's daughter, she'd met people from many different cultures. She knew that not all men were used to shaking a woman's hand.

"It's a pleasure to meet you, Mr. Saytumah. I've heard so much about you from Joseph," she said.

"Please call me Dwe. So, I finally get to meet the lovely and talented lady my son has raved about all these years. She is even lovelier than you described, Joseph," he said.

"Thank you." Sonia raised her eyebrows and looked over at Joseph. "So, he's been talking about me all these years, huh? I hope he said nice things."

"He always sings your praises," Dwe said.

Sonia smiled. She turned to Saye and extended her hand. "It's a pleasure to meet you too."

Saye took her hand, raised it to his lips and kissed it. "The pleasure is all mine." He looked into her eyes. There was no mistaking the leer in his.

Sonia wanted to laugh. She had to put a stop to this madness. She cleared her throat, gently extricated her hand and gestured toward the conference room table.

"Please, gentlemen, have a seat. Would you like something to drink? We have coffee, soda and water set up on the credenza there," she said.

"No. We are fine for now," Joseph said.

Sonia took a seat at the head of the table. "So, Mr. Saytumah, I understand you want to purchase the assets of a small shipping outfit here in the U.S."

"Yes. When I discussed this with Joseph, he told me that you negotiate these types of deals all of the time. Please tell us about that."

"Well, I've been with the firm for the past ten years. I made partner two years ago. During the time I've been here, I've negotiated all types of deals -- mergers and acquisitions, initial public offerings, asset purchases and leveraged buy-outs. The type of transaction you propose is very similar to a deal I negotiated earlier this year for another client of the firm -- a Greek shipping company that wanted to expand its presence in the U.S.," she said.

"What kinds of issues are likely to arise in connection with a transaction of this type?" Dwe asked.

"Well, in addition to the usual price and deal point issues, there will be regulatory issues having to do with you being a foreign national entering into this line of business, and tax implications as well. Fortunately, some of my partners specialize in those areas and will be able to assist us with those aspects of the deal," she said.

Dwe nodded. "Good."

"Why don't we discuss what you hope to achieve with this deal and some of the parameters? Then, we can decide how we should proceed," Sonia said.

"How we should proceed? What do you mean by that?" Dwe asked.

"Well, for starters, I need to know who will be the point person on the deal -- the one who interacts with me the most and/or takes the lead on the business side for negotiations," she said.

"For the interaction with you I appoint Joseph. Since you two are old friends, you should work well together. Also, his English is the best among the three of us. With respect to negotiations with the other side, I will be the point person," Dwe said.

Sonia stifled a groan. Under Dwe's proposed arrangement, she and Joseph would be spending a lot of time together over the next few months working on the deal. With the attraction they still felt for each other, that could lead to disastrous results. There were ethical rules prohibiting attorneys from having sexual relationships with their clients and, although her background check on Joseph and the company had revealed nothing sinister, she still didn't trust him completely. She had to find a way to convince Dwe to be the one to interact with her.

"Your English is fine, Mr. Saytumah," she said. "And since you are the lead decision maker and will be the point person in negotiations with the shipping company, may I suggest that you also be the one to interact directly with me as well? That way, there's one person in charge of both areas."

Dwe shook his head and dashed her hopes of avoiding prolonged contact with Joseph. "No. My son has had the benefit of an American education. He is much better able to handle the paperwork side of the deal. Besides, working together will give you two the opportunity to catch up."

Although his expression never changed, Sonia could swear she detected another twinkle in his eye. She wanted to laugh. The old rascal knew damned well the position he was putting her in.

Oh well. There was nothing she could do to change things short of refusing to take on the matter. And that wasn't an option. She was just going to have to do her best to keep her relationship with Joseph strictly professional.

She glanced over at him and found him watching her. He caught her eye and sent her a mischievous grin -- almost as if he'd read her thoughts. Her lips twitched with the effort not to grin back at him.

***

Two weeks later, Sonia and Joseph sat at a conference room table. It was well into the dinner hour. They'd been working on the deal all day. Used coffee cups lined up next to multiple stacks of paper on the table. Boxes piled up around the room.

Sonia marked up a large document with a red pen as she discussed her proposed changes with Joseph.

"They want to keep this provision in the agreement, but we need it taken out. Maybe if we let them keep this other provision, they'll let us get rid of that one," she said.

"I am sure my father will find a way to persuade them to see our point of view," Joseph said.

"We'll see," Sonia said.

The long hours were starting to take their toll. She yawned, stretched a little and rubbed the back of her neck.

Joseph stood up, walked behind her and started to massage her aching neck and tight shoulders.

Sonia moaned softly and felt her body relax. What he was doing felt good -- too good. It was also highly inappropriate. She stiffened.

"What are you doing?" she asked.

"I am giving you a massage. It's late and you have been working very hard for my family. When you started rubbing your neck, I realized how tired and stiff you must be from sitting in here all day and half the night," he said.

Sonia slapped his hands away. "Stop that! It's making me nervous. You're paying me to work hard for your family. You don't need to give me a massage too."

Joseph returned to his seat. "As you wish, my lady. I wouldn't want to make you nervous. Tell me -- why does my giving you a simple shoulder massage make you so nervous?"

"Never mind that." Sonia suppressed a wince. Her tone was sharper than she'd intended it to be. "Now, where were we?"

"Paragraph 107 on page 36." Joseph said.

"Good. We're almost done."

"You sound happy about that. Has it been such an ordeal working with me?"

"No. Actually, it's been kind of nice. Your father was right. We work well together. I just want to get this done for him. He said he wanted the deal closed by the beginning of next month. I'm just trying to keep us on track. Why would you ask me that?"

"Because the more time we spend together, the more tense and nervous you seem to get," he said.

"Sorry about that. I always get a little tense this far into a deal. I think it has something to do with seeing the finish line and wanting to get across it," she said.

"You need to find time to relax," he said.

"Look who's talking. From what I recall, you worked around the clock for your father's company while being a full-time student."

"But I made time to be with you, didn't I?"

"True," she said. "You did manage to find time to do that."

Memories of the time they'd spent together came flooding back. They were never very big on conversation. She looked up to find Joseph grinning at her. She released her bottom lip from the clutches of her teeth and shook her head. He was impossible.

"Okay," she said, deliberately making her tone brisk. "Let's finish this up so we can get some sleep before tomorrow morning's conference calls."

"Together or apart?"

She sent him a stern look. "Joseph, this is not the time or place for that. Besides, we went that route and failed a long time ago. Cultural differences. Remember?"

"Yes, I do remember. But who is to say we haven't grown and changed since then?" he asked.

"Look, there are ethical rules and firm policies against attorneys having romantic relationships with clients and I like my job very much. So let's focus on the deal. Alright?"

"Yes. For now."

Sonia frowned at him. It wasn't the answer she was looking for, but it would have to do. They had a lot of work to do. She'd worry about the rest later.

Chapter III

Dwe and Saye met with the vice president of the shipping company at their offices in Newark, New Jersey. They'd agreed to meet without counsel to see if they could work out the last few deal issues. Saye said little during the meeting. It was his job to intimidate the executive. He stared menacingly at the man while his father exuded charm and grace.

The executive kept throwing nervous glances in Saye's direction. Saye wanted to laugh. Americans. If a few mean glares was all it took to intimidate them, he could rack up here.

"So you see," Dwe said, "it is very important to us that we obtain full control of the company after closing. You and your father will be provided with generous retirement packages in addition to the buyout price for your shares."

With a visible effort, the executive tore his eyes away from Saye and turned to face Dwe. "We thank you for your very generous offer Mr. Saytumah, however, you must understand that my father built this company from scratch more than forty years ago. He spent most of my childhood -- hell, most of my life -- working to turn it into the successful company we are now. You can't just expect him to immediately cease all involvement with the company after the closing. Couldn't you find some way to ease him out gradually? You could, for example, let him serve on the board of directors or keep him on as a consultant. Why not take advantage of his very considerable knowledge and expertise?"

"I am afraid that will not work. It is inconsistent with both my company's business practices and those of the Liberian government. As I have explained to you, Liberia has worked very hard to obtain some measure of self-determination and independence. Having the old guard still in place after the closing would not serve to fulfill those goals. It would be a shame for this deal to fall apart over so small an issue. Why don't you take a little time to fully evaluate this new proposal with the revised compensation figures and get back to us?" Dwe asked.

"We will certainly do that," the shipping company executive said. "I am not so sure, however, that this is not a deal breaker. My father can be rather stubborn. It's the trait that's made him so successful. He never gives up."

"Then your father and I have something in common. I am sure we will be able to work this out. Not being able to close this deal would result in dire consequences to both parties. Of course, we want to avoid that at all costs," Dwe said.

He stood up. The executive stood as well. They shook hands.

Dwe and Saye left the building and stepped into the Lincoln town car waiting for them at the curb. Dwe turned to Saye. "The president of the company needs a little persuasion that it is in his best interests to close the deal on the terms we propose."

Saye nodded. "I can think of a couple of ways to accomplish that, Father. Do you have something specific in mind?"

"Yes, I do." Dwe opened his briefcase and pulled out a manila envelope. He opened it and extracted some photographs. He leafed through them until he came to one depicting a cute little blue-eyed blonde girl of no more than six years of age. He tapped the photo. "This is a picture of the president's granddaughter, Karen. She is adorable is she not? She also happens to be the daughter of the man we just met. I want you to devise a plan to convince the father and grandfather of that beautiful little girl that it is in her and their best interests to have this deal go through," he said.

Saye's eyes gleamed. "Yes, father. I believe I can do that."

Dwe looked at him sternly. "But son, make sure that you do not harm a hair on that little girl's head. Americans are very protective when it comes to little girls with blue eyes and blonde hair. We do not need to bring the full wrath of the U.S. Government down on us for overkill. Start out slow and escalate only if you need to."

Saye felt his hands curl into fists. He was so tired of being treated like an incompetent fool. His father never treated Joseph this way. "Of course, father. Must you berate me like a child? I know what to do."

Dwe nodded and patted Saye's hand. "I know, son. This is one of your specialties. That's why I saved this role just for you."

Saye smiled, pleased to finally get some acknowledgment of his abilities and the opportunity to play a role in the transaction. He would do a good job. By the time he was done, the executive would give them anything they wanted.

**

A few days later, the president of the shipping company sat at his kitchen table reading the New York Times and sipping a cup of coffee. As she did every Saturday morning, his wife walked through the front door with a basket full of unopened mail. She sat down and sifted through the envelopes, dividing up the bills from the junk mail. She picked up a manila envelope and frowned at it. "Honey."

He sighed. *Can't a man read a newspaper in piece?*

"Hmmm?" he asked.

"This is for you." She held out the envelope.

"Okay, just leave it there, dear. I'll open it later."

His wife shrugged and put the envelope down on the table in front of him. She finished sorting through the mail, discarded the junk mail and took the invoices into the den.

After she left, the executive put down the newspaper and picked up the manila envelope. He studied it and frowned. There was no label on the envelope and no return address. His name and address were neatly handwritten across the front. He opened the envelope and looked inside. There was no letter – only a few photographs. Curious, he pulled them out and looked at them.

His breath caught in his throat. They were pictures of his granddaughter – in the schoolyard, at the park, in the supermarket, in the front yard of her best friend's house. In the background of each of the photos was the same black man staring menacingly into the lens of the camera. He didn't recognize the man, but the message was clear. Those African bastards could get to his granddaughter anytime, anywhere, anyplace. He knew he couldn't take that chance.

He quickly stuffed the pictures back inside the envelope, took it to his study and shoved it into his briefcase. He then picked up the telephone to call his son.

***

Joseph, Dwe, Saye, Sonia, the shipping company executives and their counsel sat at a large wooden table in the law firm's main conference room. Bottles of champagne chilled in buckets on the credenza. Platters of fruit, cheese, shrimp, and crudités rested on ornately designed metal trays next to the champagne buckets.

The president of the shipping company executed the agreement then slid it over to Dwe and handed him the elegant gold pen. Dwe executed the agreement with a flourish and set the pen down onto the table.

"And so it is done," Sonia said. "Congratulations to all. Now let's celebrate." She signaled to the butlers standing by. They popped the champagne corks and handed out glasses of the bubbly golden liquid.

Dwe raised his glass. "I propose a toast to the future of Liberia Enterprises and the executives of Portside Marine who were gracious enough to make it possible for us to realize our dreams of owning our own shipping fleet."

"Hear hear." They raised their glasses in a toast and took sips of the champagne.

"I'd like to propose a toast to our beautiful and talented attorney who made this all possible," Joseph said. He turned to look at Sonia and raised his glass. She felt her cheeks warm as everyone else in the room followed suit.

Sonia raised her glass. "I'd like to toast my legal counterpart, Judd Nelson, for also helping to make this happen."

One of the junior lawyers from Nelson's law firm turned his laptop to face the former president of the shipping company. "The wire transfer has cleared."

The shipping company executive cleared his throat and rose from his chair. "Okay then, ladies and gentlemen. Thank you very much for everything. My daughter's engagement party is tonight and my wife will kill me if I don't get home soon. It's been a pleasure dealing with all of you."

"And you as well," Dwe said. He walked over to shake the executive's hand.

After the executives and their counsel left, Dwe turned to Sonia. "I cannot thank you enough for your guidance and leadership on this deal. You are indeed a beautiful and talented lady. I am having a grand celebration at my house this weekend to celebrate my seventieth birthday. You must come and be my guest."

"Mr. Saytumah, thank you very much for your kind words. It has been a pleasure working with you and your family on this matter. Thank you also for your gracious invitation, but I couldn't possibly take off to Liberia this weekend. Now that this deal has closed, I must turn my attention to other matters," Sonia said.

"Nonsense! You have worked very hard for us these past two months. Surely you can take a few days off to have some fun. Joseph will send his car to pick you up and take you to the airport. You will fly on my jet. It is a very long flight, but hopefully you will be comfortable enough on the plane. You will stay at our home in Monrovia," Dwe said, "for as long as you desire."

"Oh, Mr. Saytumah, I couldn't possibly impose on you to fly me to Liberia and put me up --- ."

Dwe waived his hand, cutting her off. "It is no imposition at all, my dear. Any friend of Joseph is a friend of the family. You don't want to disappoint an old man, do you? It would bring me much pleasure to have you at my birthday celebration." He walked over to Sonia and gave her a hug. She hugged him back. The old man had grown on her.

"There," he said. "It is settled. I will see you this weekend. Saye and I must go now. We are leaving for Liberia this afternoon to take care of some business we have been neglecting and to make last-minute arrangements for the celebration."

It was Saye's turn to hug Sonia. "It has been a pleasure meeting and working with you Sonia. I look forward to seeing you at the family compound this weekend."

"Have a safe trip," Sonia said.

Dwe and Saye said their goodbyes to Joseph and left.

Sonia shook her head. "Is your father always so hard to say no to?"

Joseph smiled. "You have no idea. So, where shall we go tonight to celebrate the successful culmination of this deal?"

"I thought we just finished celebrating," Sonia said.

Joseph twisted his lips. "You call this a celebration? Oh no, my lady. To celebrate properly, there must be dinner at least."

"We don't need to go out to dinner. I need to spend tonight figuring out how to gracefully let your father know that I won't be attending his birthday celebration," Sonia said.

"There is no getting out of that gracefully. If you don't come, I will never hear the end of it -- for the rest of my life. Joseph put his palms together in a prayer position in front of his chest. Please, please do not back out of the trip now that you have agreed to go."

Sonia laughed. The man was practically begging. She didn't doubt Dwe would ride Joseph if she backed out, but she couldn't just take off to Liberia for the weekend. "I didn't actually agree to go. I just stopped protesting."

Joseph pointed a finger at her. "That is the same thing, and you know it. You cannot back out now. My poor father would be devastated. It would ruin his birthday celebration. You cannot back out of dinner tonight, either. So, once again, where do you want to go? Or shall I surprise you?"

Sonia looked at him. He looked good, as usual, in his perfectly tailored business suit. She was so tired of fighting the attraction between them. He was wearing her down. And maybe a trip to an exotic land was exactly what she needed. It was a once-in-a-lifetime opportunity, really. When was she ever going to be offered a free trip to Africa in a private jet again? And now that the deal had closed, the ethical rules pertaining to intimate relationships with clients no longer applied.

She shrugged. "What the hell. We only live once. I'll go -- to Liberia and dinner."

Joseph's smile lit up the room. "Excellent. I will pick you up at your place at eight."

"Okay." She grabbed a legal pad, scribbled her home address on it, tore of the page and handed it to Joseph. "I'll see you at eight."

Joseph reached over, lifted her chin with a finger, and kissed her gently on the cheek. He then turned and walked out of the conference room.

Sonia stood there for a moment after he left, her hand covering the spot his lips had abandoned, and wondered why the kiss had moved her so much. Somehow, over the past few months, her old feelings for him had resurfaced. It was clear his feelings for her hadn't faded either.

She tried to weigh the pros and the cons of them getting together, but she didn't have enough information. Had he mellowed out as he got older or was he still the jealous and impossibly possessive guy she'd kicked to the curb all those years ago?

She had certainly mellowed out over the years. There was a good chance he had too. Except for a few instances of flirting and his attempt to give her a shoulder massage, he'd presented himself as a consummate professional during the time they'd worked together on the deal.

She shrugged. Only time would tell if they were more compatible now than they had been in college.

***

Tyrone, Tara, Naimah and Jared sat inside the dining room of the Nkrumah family mansion in Monrovia. Although Tyrone and Tara had been born in America, their family had lived in Liberia for generations. They were one of the first Americo-Liberian families to settle in Monrovia.

Tyrone and Tara spent many a summer at the mansion over the years visiting their grandparents who were wealthy and moved in the same social circles as the Saytumahs. Upon their deaths, they had left the mansion to their only daughter who, in turn left it to her children, Tyrone and Tara. Now, it served as the base of the CIA's Liberian operations.

Plans of the Saytumah family mansion were strewn across the dining room table, together with a model of the mansion and the outside grounds built to scale.

"Okay," Tara said, "we've gone over the plan and made a few operational changes. You won't be going in as our new driver. Instead, you're going in as one of the marines driving the embassy officials attending the birthday party."

Jared nodded his approval. "Smart. That way, if anything goes awry, your cover will remain intact."

"You just make sure nothing goes awry," Tyrone said.

"I got this," Jared said.

"Let's go over the plan one more time," Tara said.

Jared groaned. "We've been over the plan a thousand times already. I could recite it in my sleep."

Tara raised her eyebrows. "Recite it to me while you're awake."

"Okay. I wait for your signal. Once that comes through, I ask the servants for directions to the restroom. The second I'm out of their sight, I aim Naimah's device at the nearest camera I see and press the button."

He pointed at the map. "I take this hall all the way to the end and make a right here." He picked up a credit-card like device with a short wire extending from it. "I then use this little baby to bypass the keypad lock he has on the office door. Once inside, I turn on the computer and plug in the flash drive to upload the information."

Tyrone nodded. "The first device will enable Naimah to hack into the CCTV system and alter the video feed in the hallway outside the office so that it runs on a loop. It's important that you wait for her to give you the all clear before you go down the hall. As far as we know, they don't have a security camera inside the office."

"That makes sense," Jared said. "He probably doesn't want any of his private conversations recorded. Are we sure there are no additional security measures in his office like infrared sensors or some such thing?"

"We can't be a hundred percent sure. That's why we provided you with the infrared goggles. You should be wearing them before you enter the office to check for any sensors," Tara said. "You are to abort the mission at the first sign of trouble. I don't want you playing hero. Do you hear me?"

"Yes Tara. I hear you loud and clear," Jared said. He turned to Naimah and rolled his eyes. "I swear she sounds just like my mother sometimes."

Naimah laughed.

Chapter IV

Sonia walked down the narrow steps of the private jet and stepped onto the tarmac. A limousine was parked a few feet away. A beautiful statuesque African woman wearing an elaborate braided hairstyle and a designer dress stood next to it. She walked up to Sonia, embraced her and kissed her on the cheek.

Sonia was a little taken aback at the woman's familiarity, but her training in social situations as a senator's daughter taught her to roll with it. She knew that different cultures greeted people differently, so she gave the woman a little hug and plastered a smile on her face.

The woman pulled back and returned the smile. "Welcome to Liberia. My name is Fatima. I am the Minister's personal assistant. You must be Sonia."

"Yes. It is a pleasure to meet you," Sonia said.

"And you as well. I've heard so much about you. Our ride is right over here." She gestured toward the limousine.

They walked over to the limousine and climbed in. Men loaded Sonia's luggage into the trunk, then they were off.

"So, have you ever been to Liberia before?" Fatima asked.

"No. This is my first time. I've actually never been to Africa before."

"No? How did you meet the Saytumahs?"

"Well, Joseph and I met in college many years ago and I just recently represented their company in a business deal."

Fatima raised her eyebrows. "You've known Joseph for so long and he has never invited you to his home?"

Sonia smiled. "Oh, he invited me. I just didn't accept the invitation. But when Dwe asked me to attend his birthday celebration this weekend, I couldn't refuse. He's a hard man to say no to."

"Yes. That is very true," Fatima said.

"You speak English very well. Were you educated in America?" Sonia asked.

"Yes. My family is Americo-Liberian. We are descended from the freed slaves who started this country. Part of my family still lives in America, so I attended Rutgers University in New Jersey. My parents are old friends and political allies of the Saytumahs. After I graduated, the Minister hired me to be his personal assistant," Fatima said.

"I see. Well Rutgers is a good school. It's also a big party school. It must have been something of a culture shock to go there," Sonia said.

"I enjoyed it very much and received a very good education," Fatima said. After a moment of silence, she changed the subject. "Since this is your first time visiting Liberia, let me tell you a little about our history. Liberia is a very poor country. We have had two civil wars in the past thirty years. In the last civil war, much of the country's infrastructure was destroyed – most notably, the water plant facilities. There is still no running water in portions of the country. That has made it very difficult for the country to rebuild and to function."

"Yes. I read about that. How did you function with no running water?" Sonia asked.

"The families that are better off are able to have fresh water delivered to their properties. My heart goes out to the poorer families though. With the help of aid from America and other countries, we are slowly starting to rebuild. So far, the rebuilding has mostly taken place in Monrovia and the larger cities. There are still pockets of unrest in the countryside," Fatima said.

"Unrest? What do you mean by unrest?" Sonia asked.

"There are reports of rebels making trouble in some of the villages outside of Monrovia. The government sends troops to deal with it. Also, incidents of rape have increased in some areas," Fatima said.

"Wow. That sounds a little scary." Sonia sent an uneasy glance out of the limousine's windows. "Are you sure we're safe?"

Fatima put a reassuring hand on Sonia's arm. "Oh yes. You are under the protection of the Minister. You have nothing to fear. Just be sure to follow the instructions of your escorts and you will be fine."

"The Minister? Oh, you mean Dwe. I keep forgetting that he's the Minister of Internal Affairs here. I guess I think of him more as a client and as Joseph's father," Sonia said.

Fatima raised her eyebrows. "I see. We have arrived. Welcome to the Saytumah family compound."

The limousine pulled up to a set of gates set in a high stone wall that seemed to go on for blocks. The gates opened automatically and they entered the grounds. It was a sprawling and lushly landscaped property.

They drove around a circular driveway up to a large mansion. Armed guards discreetly walked the compound wearing khaki pants and crisp button down shirts. Small white Secret Service-like earpieces were visible in their ears.

The limousine stopped in front of the mansion and one of the guards opened the door on Sonia's side. She stepped out of the vehicle and followed Fatima to the entrance of the mansion. As they arrived, a short young African woman dressed in a crisp black and white maid's uniform opened the door for them.

Sonia and Fatima stepped through the door and into a beautifully decorated foyer.

Fatima turned to Sonia and spoke in a brisk tone. "Welcome to the Saytumah family home. I have some work that I need to complete for the Minister. The celebration begins at eight o'clock. Yani here will take you to your room. She will return at eight to escort you to the hall where the party will take place."

Sonia was a bit taken aback at the change in Fatima's demeanor, however, she had very little time to process the emotion before Joseph entered the foyer, walked right up to her, grabbed her by the shoulders and planted a huge kiss on her lips.

Sonia felt her heart skip a beat. "Well hello."

"Hello, my dear," he said.

They stood there for a moment smiling at each other while Fatima and Yani watched them.

Joseph turned to them. "Thank you, Fatima. I believe my father is looking for you. Yani, please take Sonia's bags to her room."

Fatima turned on her heel and left the foyer without another word. Yani signaled for a guard to pick up Sonia's bags and followed him out.

Joseph turned back to Sonia. "Would you like a tour of the house?"

"I would love one," she said. "Are you sure I'm not keeping you away from more important matters?"

"Nothing is more important. Right this way, my lady." He took her arm and led her out of the foyer.

***

At eight o'clock on the dot, Yani knocked on Sonia's door and escorted her to the hall where the birthday celebration would take place. Sonia followed her through ornate wooden double doors a surprisingly large hall.

The room was decorated as if for a wedding. Tables set up with fine china and beautiful centerpieces composed of exotic-looking white flowers were scattered throughout the room. A long rectangular table stood on a raised platform at one end of the hall; a small podium with a microphone was set up at the table's midpoint.

Servants in uniforms milled about putting finishing touches on everything. Joseph, Saye and Dwe stood just inside the door wearing tuxedos. They were involved in what appeared to be an intense discussion.

Yani cleared her throat. "Announcing Ms. Sonia Johnson."

The men abruptly ceased their conversation, plastered smiles on their faces and turned to greet Sonia. Dwe walked toward her with open arms. He hugged her and kissed her on each cheek. "Sonia! I am so happy to have you here at my party. Welcome. I trust the journey was not too difficult?"

"Difficult? It was wonderful. That was the first time I ever traveled on a private jet. I'm afraid you have quite ruined me for commercial air travel. Even first class doesn't hold a candle to a jet that has shower facilities and couches on which to sleep."

"A woman as smart and beautiful as you should be spoiled," Dwe said.

Saye approached Sonia and gave her a hug and a kiss. "Welcome, Sonia. Have you had a tour of the house yet?"

"Yes. Joseph was kind enough to take me around earlier. Your family has a beautiful home."

Saye grinned at her. "Thank you. I bet my brother was only too happy to show you around. Did he offer to show you his bedroom as well?"

"That is quite enough, brother." Joseph stepped in, took Sonia by the hands and gave her the once over. "You look beautiful as always."

"You know," she said, "I'm going to have the biggest head with all the compliments I'm getting tonight."

Joseph squeezed her hands gently and let go. "We are only telling the truth. You will join my family at the head table and sit next to me."

Sonia nodded. "I see there are at least a hundred place settings here. Who else is coming to the party?"

"President Sirleaf will be here, other ministers appointed by her, diplomats and friends and family from all over the world. The mansion is full tonight with our guests as is the main hotel downtown," he said.

"There's a downtown area in Monrovia? I'd love to see that," she said.

"I will take you on a tour tomorrow," he said.

"Do you hang out downtown when you come home to visit?" she asked.

"No. Much of our socializing is done at friends' houses," he said.

Yani entered the room again and announced the arrival of Tyrone and Tara Nkrumah. Saye, Joseph and Dwe greeted them warmly.

Joseph introduced Sonia. "Sonia, Tyrone and Tara are longtime friends of the family. We practically grew up together. Tyrone, Tara, meet Sonia Johnson."

Tara raised her eyebrows. "Oh, so you're the woman Joseph has been ranting about all these years. He finally got you to come to Liberia, I see. What a pleasure to finally meet you." She shook Sonia's hand.

Tyrone glanced at his sister, rolled his eyes and extended his hand and a warm smile to Sonia. "Don't listen to her. She's always getting into other people's business. It's nice to meet you, Sonia. Any friend of the Saytumah family is a friend of ours." He enveloped her hand in his large one and shook it.

Tara punched her brother on the arm. He rubbed it good-naturedly.

"So, how long will you be in Liberia?" Tara asked.

"Oh. I'm just here for the weekend. I return to the states on Monday," Sonia said.

Tara turned to Joseph. "You must bring her over to our house tomorrow. We'll have a little dinner party and hang out."

"That sounds like a great idea. What time should we come over?" Joseph asked.

"How about seven o'clock?"

"Seven it is then," Joseph said. "Yani will escort you to your table." He took Sonia by the hand, led her to the head table and seated her. He then rejoined his father and brother at the front door to greet guests.

Sonia sipped a glass of wine and chatted with Joseph's aunt who sat next to her at the head table. The woman practically interrogated Sonia about her background.

More people entered the room, were announced, and greeted by Joseph, Saye and Dwe as they entered; servants then ushered them off to tables.

President Sirleaf was the last to arrive. Dwe, Joseph and Saye escorted her to the head table and seated her next to Dwe.

***

Tara watched Joseph walk up to the podium. The evening's program was about to begin. Her hands were already in her lap, so no-one noticed when she signaled Jared. She put her finger over the large stone of the ring she wore on her right hand and pressed down. The circuit inside sent an electronic signal to Jared's com.

Joseph thanked everyone for attending the event and introduced the president of Liberia who gave a short speech. At the end of it, she congratulated Dwe on his seventieth birthday and his long and dedicated service to the people of Liberia.

After she took her seat, Dwe stood up and approached the podium. "First, I want to thank President Sirleaf for taking the time to attend my birthday celebration. I also want to congratulate her on the excellent job she is doing to rebuild the country after so many years of civil war. Thanks to her, women and children are safer in this country, relations with the U.S. and other countries have improved, civil unrest is at an all-time low and there is finally a light at the end of the tunnel for Liberia. Second, I want to thank all of you for attending. I consider you to be among my closest friends and family and it warms my heart to have you here. The time for speeches has now passed. Let us eat, drink, and be merry. After dinner, we will clear the floor for dancing. We have brought in a very special musical guest for your pleasure."

The crowd clapped and cheered and dinner was served. Tyrone caught Tara's eye. She gave him an almost imperceptible nod then turned to engage the woman next to her in conversation. She heard Tyrone laugh at some joke. She hoped Jared got the signal.

***

Jared and the other drivers milled about in a small parlor located next to the servants' quarters. A dinner buffet was set up for them. Some of the drivers held lively debates on Liberian politics and other issues. Others played cards or dominoes. The marine drivers kept mostly to themselves. Jared got himself a plate of food and sat down with them. He ate while they talked. One of the marines decided to include him in their conversation.

"Hi. I'm John," he said, holding out his hand.

"Mike," Jared said. He shook the soldier's hand.

"This is Jerry and Frank." John pointed at the other marine drivers. Jared shook their hands too.

"You're brand spanking new here, aren't you Marine? So, where were you stationed prior to coming here?" John asked.

"I was at Quantico," Jared said.

He had said the first place that popped into his head. He hoped none of the other marines had been stationed there.

"Quantico? That's a pretty cushy assignment. Who did you piss off to get stationed here?" John asked.

Jared smiled. "Let's just say I got caught in bed with the wrong lieutenant's wife."

The marines laughed. "Oh man. I hope it was worth it."

Jared grinned. "It sure was."

A tone sounded in his earpiece. It was time for him to move. He got up. "Excuse me for a minute. I've got to see a man about a horse."

He walked across the parlor into the kitchen area. He stopped the first servant he ran into and asked for directions to the restroom. The servant pointed across the kitchen to a doorway. Jared thanked him.

He stepped through the kitchen door into a hallway. It was empty. He looked up and scanned the walls for surveillance cameras. He found one so discreetly tucked behind a lamp that he almost missed it. He turned to the right, away from the camera and took out what appeared to be a pack of cigarettes.

He walked down the hall toward the bathroom, aimed the top of the pack of cigarettes behind him in the direction of the camera, and pressed the button in the device. He then walked into the bathroom and shut the door behind him. He scanned the bathroom for hidden cameras. Seeing none, he put the cigarettes away. He flushed the toilet and ran some water in the sink.

"At least you wash your hands," Naimah said in his ear.

He grinned. "Yes, my mother taught me well."

Naimah sighed. "The things we have to go through for our country. You're good to go. I'm in. I have control of the system and I'm running the footage outside the study on a loop."

"I knew you were more than just a pretty face," Jared said.

"Lucky for you that's true," Naimah said. "Now go."

Jared opened the door and looked up and down the hallway. It was empty. He made a left turn and walked to the end of the corridor. Flattening himself against the wall, he peered around the corner. No guards were in sight. He quickly made his way down the hall until he came to a door with a keypad next to it. He reached into his jacket pocket and pulled out the keypad scrambler. He plugged one end of the device into the keypad. Numbers flashed across the screen for what seemed like forever. He glanced up and down the hallway. "What is taking this damned thing so long?"

"The keypad has a ten-digit encryption key," Naimah said.

Finally, the flashing stopped and the last digit went stationary on the device. He put his hand on the doorknob and turned it. The door opened. He disengaged the keypad device, reached into his other jacket pocket, pulled out a pair of infrared goggles, and slipped them on. He then eased the door open a couple of inches and peered inside. Not seeing any infrared beams, he stepped inside and closed the door behind him.

A lamp sitting on the large desk provided a little light. With his back to the door, he took off the goggles and scanned the room for cameras and alarm boxes. He saw none. "I'm in."

He crossed the room and walked over to the desk. Squatting down, he located the power switch on the computer. He turned it on and plugged the drive in.

"Okay, it's working," Naimah said. "The upload should begin in a minute."

"Good." Jared rifled through the papers on the desk while he waited and came across a file containing plans for some building. Upon closer inspection, he realized they were plans for the Presidential mansion. He extracted a miniature camera from his pocket and shot pictures of the documents. When he finished, he glanced at his watch. Three minutes had elapsed. "Are we almost done?"

"No." Naimah sounded perplexed. "I don't know what's happening. My computer says the device is gathering information, but I'm just not getting the upload. Something must be blocking the signal."

Jared heard the tapping of computer keys on her end. "Should I abort?"

"Not yet," Naimah said. "Let me try one more thing."

"Okay, but make it fast. I don't have a good feeling about this."

***

Inside the ballroom, the dinner dishes were cleared away. Two servants brought out a huge birthday cake on a stand and rolled it next to the head table. It was a multi-tier cake done up in a design as elaborate as any wedding cake Sonia had ever seen.

The guests sang happy birthday songs to Dwe in both English and a Liberian dialect. The Minister looked pleased as he blew out the candles. During the singing, Tara excused herself from the table and slipped out a side door onto a terrace. She extracted an earpiece from her clutch and put it in her ear.

"Status," she said.

"Jared is still in Dwe's study," Naimah said. "We're having trouble uploading the information from the computer. I'm trying to figure out what the problem is. Everything looks normal on my end."

"Jared, can you hear me?" Tara asked.

"Loud and clear," he said.

"What does it look like on your end?" she asked.

"It's quiet in here. I didn't see any security roaming the halls on my way in. There was no alarm system or other security system in Dwe's study as far as I could tell. The computer screen is blank. I don't know why the information isn't uploading. Maybe there's something wrong with the drive."

Tara was silent for a moment as she decided what to do. On one hand, this was the best opportunity they'd had to get the data. On the other hand, it would be easy to lose track of the Saytumahs now that the program was over. Jared was taking a huge risk. Plus, she didn't have a good feeling about the mission. "Abort. I don't like it."

"Are you sure?" Jared asked. "It will be a long time before we get another opportunity like this."

"Yes. I'm sure. Abort," she said.

"Roger that," Jared said.

***

Tyrone watched a guard enter the ballroom, walk up to the head table and whisper in Dwe's ear. Dwe turned and caught Saye's eye. When Saye approached, Dwe whispered in his ear. Saye nodded, straightened and headed toward the door. He motioned for a guard to follow him.

Tyrone excused himself from the table and joined Tara on the terrace. "Something's happening. Saye just left the hall with a guard. What's the status?"

Tara turned to look at him and a knot formed in Tyrone's gut. She looked tense. She never looked tense.

"There's a problem with the uplink," she said. "I told Jared to abort. He should be leaving Dwe's office now." She touched her earpiece. "Jared, tell me you got out of there. Saye just left the ballroom. We believe he's coming to you."

Tyrone slipped in his earpiece just in time to hear Jared curse.

"I was trying to give Naimah one more minute to fix the uplink." Jared said. "Naimah, how does it look out there?"

"Let me check," she said. "Oh my God."

"What do you mean? Don't say that," Jared said.

"What is it, Naimah?" Sonia asked.

"Armed guards are headed to Dwe's study from all directions. Saye and one of the guards are two corridors away coming from the direction of the ballroom. Another contingent is one corridor away coming from the other direction. Jared, there are no windows in the study. You need to get out of there right now. There's a room two doors down on the left. The plans show it has a terrace," she said.

"Move!" Tara said.

"Moving," Jared said.

"Hurry," Naimah said. "They're going to have a visual on you in twenty seconds."

Tyrone could hear Jared moving quietly. There was a pause, and he could visualize Jared picking the locks. He heard the quiet closing of a door and barely made out the sound of Jared's footsteps as he crossed the room. He heard the sound of a sliding glass door quietly opening and closing and then there was silence. He couldn't even hear the sound of Jared's breath.

"Naimah, are you sure this is the only way out?" Jared asked.

"It's the only one I can see at the moment," she said. "Why?"

"I'm looking down at a sheer drop of at least a hundred feet into the sea," he said.

"What? Oh that's right, the Saytumah family mansion is on beachfront property. That whole side of the house overlooks the water," she said.

"I don't see any beach," he said. "Just a whole lot of rocks."

"Hold your position for now," Tara said.

Chapter V

Saye and the guard walked down the corridor to Dwe's study. He opened the door and stepped in, the guard following closely behind. The room was empty.

He headed over to his father's desk and checked the computer. It was turned on. He checked the security program on the computer and saw that a U.S.B. drive had been attached to the computer and then removed. He sat there for a moment stroking his beard.

Who would dare to do this? It must be the Americans.

He picked up the telephone handset and dialed the security office. The head of security answered.

"Sir?"

"I want you to confirm the whereabouts of all the American diplomatic personnel and their staff on premises immediately. Let me know if any are unaccounted for." Saye replaced the handset and turned to the guards who were with him. "Someone has been in here using this computer. I want you to do a room by room search of the house and the grounds.

You are looking for anyone who doesn't belong here and any guest who is out of place."

***

Jared waited on the terrace and tried to figure out his next move. He heard Naimah's voice in his ear.

"Guards are now everywhere. It appears that Saye has ordered a grid-by-grid search of the mansion, and a headcount," she said.

"Oh no," Tara said.

"Jared, they're checking the room across from yours now. Your room is next," Naimah said.

Jared looked down at the sea crashing into the rocks below. He had to do something. He couldn't let the guards find him. He threw his leg over the edge of the balcony, climbed over the rail, and lowered himself until he dangled from balcony floor by his fingertips. From his precarious position, he heard the guards enter the apartment. A moment later, he heard the terrace doors open. One of the guards stepped out onto the terrace. Jared held his breath. After a moment, the guard stepped back into the apartment and closed the terrace doors. A few moments later, Jared heard the door to the suite open and close.

"They've left the apartment and cleared the corridor," Naimah said.

Jared breathed a sigh of relief. Maybe he'd get out of here alive after all. One thing was for sure, he'd always take mission briefings seriously in the future. He'd no idea how nerve-wracking fieldwork could be. Tara's voice interrupted his thoughts.

"Get out of there and get back to the limo," she said.

"Yes ma'am." Jared pulled himself up the side of the balcony and climbed back onto the terrace. He then walked over to the terrace doors and tried to open them. They were locked. "Um, I'm having a slight problem following that order."

"What problem?" Tara asked.

"The guard locked the terrace door," he said.

"Well, can't you pick the lock?" Tara asked.

"No. There's no keyhole. It's locked with a deadbolt on the inside. I'm either going to have to break the glass in the door or find another way inside," he said.

Tara groaned. "This is a disaster. What else can go wrong with this mission? Don't answer that. Naimah, is there anyone in the corridor outside the apartment?"

"No," Naimah said.

"Okay," Tara said. "Jared, you're good to go."

Jared looked around for something he could use to break the glass in the terrace door. He settled on a wooden chair. He picked it up, raised it over his head and brought it down against the glass. The door shattered with a loud crash. Jared waited a moment listening for any sign someone had heard the glass break. Hearing nothing, he stepped into the apartment, strode across the living room and reached out to open the door leading to the hallway. He froze when he heard Naimah's voice in his ear.

"Oh no," she said.

"What?" he asked.

"Saye just stepped out of the study into the hall and he has a gun," Naimah said.

"I thought you said there was no-one in the corridor," he said.

"There wasn't. He must have been in the study," Naimah said. "He probably heard the glass breaking. Oh my God, he's pulling out a key."

Jared knew he was about to be caught. He couldn't afford to be captured; there was too much at stake. He knew what he had to do. He turned around, ran to the terrace and climbed over the balcony ledge. He looked down at the sea below and tried to figure out the best way to jump and survive. "Listen, we all know I can't let them capture me. If they do, we run the risk of compromising your cover. I can't let that happen. I'm going to jump off the terrace and hope for the best. I suggest you have the embassy send over another driver for my limo."

"No Jared," Tara said. "Don't jump. Are you crazy? We'll find a way to get you out of there."

Jared heard the apartment door open. "It's too late."

He had run out of time and options. Saying a silent prayer, he let go of the balcony rail.

***

Tara heard a rush of air, a loud splash, and then silence.

"Jared. Jared!" she said.

Tyrone grabbed her by the arm. "Keep your voice down."

Jared didn't respond. The air felt like it was being pressed from Tara's lungs. *Dear God let him be all right.*

Tyrone reached out and squeezed her shoulder. "Sis, there'll be time to worry later. Right now, we have to do damage control. I'll call the embassy and arrange for another driver to take Jared's place. Naimah, I need for you to arrange a search for him. We need to find him before Saye does. If they find him, it'll cause an international incident. We can't have that. We won't be able to continue our work and Jared's sacrifice will have been in vain. Tara, you and I have to go back in there, maintain our cover and act as if we don't have a care in the world. Can you handle that?"

Tara stared at him and wondered if she could, then a cold rage slammed into her burning out the worry and the grief. She'd be damned if she'd let the bastards win. "Yes. Of course."

"Good girl." Tyrone nodded his approval. He pulled out his cell phone and called the embassy, then he and Tara walked back into the hall, took their seats, and engaged the other guests in conversation.

***

After dinner, the R&B diva Regina Belle joined the band onstage.

Sonia turned to Joseph. "I can't believe your father flew Regina Belle in to perform at his birthday party."

"Actually, that was my birthday present to him," Joseph said.

Sonia gaped at him. "You arranged this?"

Joseph nodded, then extended a hand. "Shall we dance?"

"Oh, but this is a slow song," Sonia said.

"Exactly." he said.

He led her onto the dance floor and pulled her into his arms. They fit well together, and she found herself melting into him. Three songs later, he led her off the dance floor and out into the gardens. It was a warm, clear night. The moon seemed impossibly large and the stars exceptionally bright as he led her into a quiet corner of the garden. A slight breeze carried the scent of exotic blooms.

"It's so beautiful out here and it smells wonderful. What flower is that?" she asked.

"That would be the night-blooming jasmine. It used to be my mother's favorite flower; however, the most beautiful flower out here tonight is you." He took her into his arms and kissed her. Lust snaked through her belly. It felt like old times. She returned the kiss.

"Come with me." He took her by the hand and led her into the mansion through a side door. They entered an office. He led her through it into a hallway and down the hall.

"Where are we going?" Sonia asked.

"Somewhere we can have some privacy."

"You're not going to give me a tour of your bedroom like your brother suggested, are you?" she asked.

"Yes. For once my inappropriate brother was correct," he said.

"Don't worry, I won't tell him he was right. You'll never hear the end of it," she said.

"I appreciate that." His dry tone made her giggle.

He led her by the hand to his bedroom. When they got there, he pulled her inside and kissed her. His lips were rough, demanding. His hands gripped her hair and pulled her head back to give him greater access.

Yeah, just like old times. Her fingers dug into his shoulders almost of their own volition. She could feel his hardened manhood pressing into her belly. Desire shot like a flame down her belly to her pubic area causing her to moan. He broke off the kiss and pulled her across the room, to stand next to the king-sized bed. He slid his fingers under the straps of her dress and pushed them over her shoulders. He then got behind her and unzipped it. It fell into a pool at her feet.

He pushed her hair to one side and sank his teeth lightly into the back of her neck. It was erotic and, at the same time, it made her feel vulnerable. She shivered. His pulled her back against him and began playing with her breasts through her bra. He reached inside her bra and began pinching and rolling her nipples between his fingers. She arched her back and moaned; the movement pressed his erection firmly against her.

He let her go, unhooked her bra and pushed it over her shoulders. It joined her dress on the floor. He planted kisses from the nape of her neck all the way down her spine. He then gripped her hips and sank his teeth lightly into her behind. The tiny pain made her gasp. He took two fingers, pushed them into the folds of her vagina and massaged her clitoris. What he was doing felt so damned good that she groaned and writhed, spread her legs a little wider, and rubbed herself against his hand like a cat.

He withdrew his fingers, scooped her up and tossed her onto the bed. She landed on her back. As she lay there trying to catch her breath, he stripped off his clothes and crawled between her legs. He yanked her legs open, put his head between them and proceeded to drive her insane with his mouth. He sucked and gently nibbled until she was writhing in ecstasy. After she reached orgasm, her girly bits became very sensitive. She tried to get away from him but he was relentless. He pinned her down and continued his efforts until she thought she'd go mad.

After she came for the second time, he put his hand around his engorged member, moved up on the bed and drove it into her. Pleasure and pain had her crying out, as he began thrusting in and out of her. He gripped each of her legs under the knee, pushed them upward toward her shoulders and continued pounding away. She could feel herself being stretched to the limit. Then he found her g-spot and all discomfort melted away as pleasure took over. He hit it again and again. This time, the orgasm was so strong that she could swear she went blind for a moment.

She gasped for air.

He didn't stop even after she came down from the orgasm. He reached down and began playing with her again. His hard pounding and his fingers on her supersensitive flesh sent aftershocks through her until, finally, he came. He roared, dug his knees into the bed, and ground his hips into her.

Afterwards, they lay there quietly, their arms wrapped around each other and drifted off to sleep. He woke her up in the middle of the night. This time, he took her from behind. It felt like he was pounding into her very soul.

***

Jared didn't make it.

Tara, Tyrone and Naimah sat in the living room of the Nkrumah family home. Tara's head ached and her eyes felt swollen and irritated. She wiped at the tears on her face. Tyrone's arm around her shoulders provided some comfort. She knew he also felt the pain of Jared's death.

Neither one of them had ever lost an agent before. It was a minor miracle actually. The Agency had high rates of turnover -- for good reason. It was dangerous work they did -- important work, but still dangerous. Knowing that did nothing to lessen the pain and guilt Tara felt. She sagged against her brother. His arm tightened around her shoulders.

Tara glanced at Naimah. Her usually happy face was streaked with tears and pinched with misery. She sat there in silence, her shoulders slumped, just staring out into space.

She needs for me to be a leader -- to be strong -- Tara thought, and straightened, dislodging Tyrone's arm. She grabbed some tissues from the box he had placed on the dining room table and blew her nose. Then she looked at Naimah. "What happened?" she asked.

"It was all my fault," Naimah said. "I ran a diagnostic after it all went down. The best I can tell, Jared tripped a silent alarm when he turned on the computer. That must have alerted the guards. By the time we were able to alert him that the guards were coming, it was too late. He had no choice but to go into that suite. When you asked me to check the corridor, I did. It was empty. But I lost track of Saye. I didn't know he was still in the study. If I had known that, I would have told Jared not to break that terrace door and he'd still be alive." Naimah covered her face with her hands.

Tara rose from the couch, walked over to Naimah and touched her arm. "No Naimah, you don't know that. It's not your fault. We checked that place inside and out. There was no way we could have known about the silent alarm. And with so many cameras to monitor it's no wonder you lost track of Saye. None of us thought he'd still be in the study – not you, not me, and not Jared. Jared knew what the risks were. He knew we couldn't afford to let him get caught. He did what he had to do."

Naimah was silent for a moment. "I never lost an agent before."

"It may be your first time, ours too, but unfortunately, it won't be our last," Tara said. "Now look, we have to report this fiasco to Ben. Let's get our game faces on and our stories straight."

Naimah nodded. "I'm going to go make some repairs to my face." She got up and left the room.

Tyrone stared at Tara.

"What?" she asked.

"That was a nice little speech you gave Naimah and good advice. Just make sure you heed it too."

Tara walked back over to the couch, sat down next to her brother and hung her head. "I can't help but feel responsible. I hand-picked him for this operation and now he's dead. I can't help but wonder if he would have gotten locked on that terrace if he had a little more experience."

Tyrone patted her on the shoulder. "I know it won't do any good to say this because you already know it, but I'm going to say it anyway. It's not your fault. He was good and he was ready. In hindsight, I don't see what other options he had. He just ran into some bad luck. You and I both know that happens all the time on operations. Sometimes experience and preparation can help you work through a run of bad luck and sometimes you're just fucked."

"I know that. You're right. It doesn't make it any easier." She sighed. "I guess I'd better fix my face too, before we videoconference with Ben."

Chapter VI

Sonia looked out of the windows of the limousine as it slowly drove through downtown Monrovia. The streets were filled with traffic and pedestrians. Taxicabs crammed with up to six passengers -- two in the front and four in the back -- lined up for miles. People pushing wheelbarrows and carrying bundles on their heads headed down the street. Vendors manning tables and carts hawked their wares and haggled with potential customers.

Old, decrepit buildings stood next to brand new ones. Cranes towered over half-built structures. As they approached the outer skirts of the city, the traffic became lighter.

"What was Liberia like before all those years of civil war?" she asked.

"It was much nicer back then. There were many more restaurants, nightclubs and other entertainment venues. Downtown Monrovia was a hot spot. There was an active tourist industry back then as well and many luxury hotels. It was a very different place," he said.

"Do you think Liberia will ever be like that again?" Sonia asked.

"I think so. With the help of the Americans and China, and strong leadership, Liberia will rise again. As you can see, we have already started to rebuild," he said.

The limousine pulled up to a large wrought iron gate set in a stone wall. The driver rolled down his window and pressed an electronic call button. The gates opened and the limousine pulled up a long driveway to a mansion.

The door to the mansion opened and Tyrone stepped out. Sonia and Joseph climbed out of the limousine. While Joseph and Tyrone gave each other man hugs and pounded each other on the back, Sonia looked around. The Nkrumahs' property was almost as impressive as the Saytumah family compound. It was a sprawling estate with meticulously landscaped grounds. The mansion itself was large and built in a Spanish Tudor style. Armed guards patrolled the property.

Tyrone turned to Sonia, embraced her and kissed her on both cheeks. "Sonia, I'm so glad you were able to make it to our place before returning to America. Come in. Tara is dying to see you and engage in girl talk."

Sonia smiled. "I wouldn't have missed it for the world. What a beautiful property."

"Thank you. Our family has lived on this land for more than a hundred years. We had to abandon it for a time during the civil wars, but were able to return and rebuild. Let's get you inside so Tara can give you a tour of the place."

Tyrone led them through the foyer and into a drawing room where Tara waited for them. She rushed forward to dispense hugs and kisses. "Sonia! It's so good to see you. Joseph, you must tell the Minister that his birthday party was the best one ever! I could not believe the decorations. And Regina Belle? What could he possibly do to top that? I cannot wait until his eightieth birthday party."

Joseph laughed. "His eightieth birthday party? God bless him that he should live so long."

"Ha! As ornery as he is, he should live well past ninety," Tyrone said.

"Let us hope and pray," Joseph said.

Tara turned to Sonia. "Come with me. I'll take you on a tour of the mansion."

"That would be great," Sonia said.

"Joseph, I am going to take your girl away for a bit. You can live without her for a little while, right?" Tara smiled at him.

"Well, maybe for a little while," he said. He grabbed Sonia by the shoulders and drew her in to plant a quick kiss on her lips.

Out of the corner of her eye, Sonia saw Tara smirk. She could feel the blush warming her cheeks.

Tara took Sonia by the hand and led her out of the drawing room. "So, how long have you known Joseph?"

"Oh, we met during my senior year in college. We dated briefly back then, but it didn't work out.

We lost touch for a while. Then he just showed up at my law firm out of the blue and hired me to represent his company in a business transaction."

"How interesting that he just showed up at your firm after all those years. What sort of transaction was it?" Tara asked.

"The Saytumahs' company acquired a small shipping enterprise," Sonia said.

"I see." Tara slid open a pair of heavy ornate wooden doors and gestured. "This is the living room."

Sonia stepped into the room and took a good look. It could have been a page right out of *Better Homes and Gardens*. "Oh! What a lovely room. Just look at those beautiful antiques. Do you spend much time in here?"

"Not really. We use it more for formal entertaining. I spend most of my time in the family room or the entertainment room."

"You have an entertainment room?" Sonia asked.

"Yes. We have a private movie theater, a surround sound stereo system, a large selection of DVD's and CD's, video games, board games, computers with internet access and books. Without those things, Tyrone and I would probably lose our minds. Since the civil war, there are not a lot of entertainment options here in Liberia," Tara said.

"Joseph told me that this is your family home. Do your parents live here as well?" Sonia asked.

"No. This was our grandparents' home. When they died, my mother inherited it. She left it to me and Tyrone," Tara said. She waved a hand. "But enough about me, I want to know all about you – the woman who appears to have captured our good friend's heart. So, it looks like you and Joseph have rekindled your relationship."

Sonia couldn't stop the smile that spread across her lips. "Is it that obvious?"

"I see the way you two look at each other -- especially the way he looks at you," Tara said.

"Really? How does he look at me?"

"As if you were the last woman on Earth. I've never seen him look at another woman like that. So, is it serious?"

"I don't know. It's much too early to tell," Sonia said.

The grandfather clock in the corner of the living room began to chime. Tara glanced at it.

"Oh, look at the time. We'd better get back. It's time for dinner."

***

Later that evening, Tara and Tyrone sat alone in the drawing room. Sonia and Joseph had left.

"Did you find out anything new from Joseph?" Tara asked.

"Not really. When we talked about politics, he just talked about how Liberia needs strong leadership.

What about you? What kind of girl talk did you have with the lovely and oh-so-built Sonia?" Tyrone asked.

"Careful. Joseph may have your eyes cut out with a machete for even looking at his woman. Have you seen the way he looks at her?" Tara asked.

"Yes, but when I asked him about her, he just said they were old friends from college," Tyrone said.

"They were more than old friends. They dated in college. She said they lost touch with each other for a while and that he recently just showed up out of the blue at her law firm. He hired her to represent the Saytumahs in their acquisition of a small shipping company," Tara said.

"Oh ho. Owning a fleet of ships should come in handy for purposes of smuggling guns into Liberia. We need to get the details of that transaction. It appears that Joseph has an agenda as far as Sonia is concerned. I don't think it's a coincidence he just showed up at her firm after all these years. How much do you think she knows about their operation?" Tyrone asked.

"Not much, if anything at all. Naimah found nothing out of the ordinary when she searched Sonia's apartment. I think their relationship is still in the early stages. She doesn't seem sure of where they're headed and we found no indication she had a serious boyfriend at her place. There were no pictures, no second toothbrush, no men's clothing in her closet. Also, there was a drawer full of single girl provisions in her nightstand," Tara said.

Tyrone grinned. "Thank you for that. I'll have sweet dreams tonight."

Tara rolled her eyes. Men were so predictable, her brother no exception.

"We need to figure out exactly what the Saytumahs are up to. Keep your head in the game, bro. Keep your head in the game."

***

Joseph walked into his father's study and found him sitting behind his desk. He had always liked this room. It was a man's room, decorated in leather and dark wood. It was also the room of a scholar. Wooden bookshelves filled with hardcover books lined the walls. Most of the books were first and second editions of the classics. No trashy paperback novels for his father. He would have a room like this one day.

He looked at his father. More gray appeared in his hair than before, deep lines had etched themselves into his face on the sides of his mouth, and his pallor was a little off. His father did not look well. He wanted to ask him about it, but held his tongue. His father clearly did not want to discuss the issue of his health. He made a note to speak to the family doctor before he headed back to the States. "Hello father. Saye told me you wanted to see me."

Dwe put down his pen and smiled at Joseph. "Yes, my son. I see that you and Sonia are getting along very well this time."

Joseph smiled. "Yes. We are."

"Good. She will be a great asset to the family. Don't let her get away this time."

"I know, father. I don't intend to. I am going to ask her to marry me when we get back."

Dwe nodded. "Excellent. But don't move too quickly. Give it a little time. American women like to be courted first." He rose from his seat and approached the portrait of Joseph's mother which hung on the wall behind the desk. He examined the portrait for a moment before reaching behind the left bottom corner of the picture frame and pushing a hidden button. A portion of the wall slid aside to reveal a safe. He opened it and took out a jewelry box.

Curious, Joseph joined his father behind the desk. Dwe turned to face him and opened the box to reveal two platinum rings. One of the rings had a large diamond in its center. The other ring was a wedding band. Smaller diamonds dotted it at regular intervals. The brilliant stones gleamed in the light of the study.

"I want you to have this," Dwe said. "It was your mother's wedding ring set. I was going to pass them on to Saye, but I fear he will never get married and produce an heir to carry on the family name."

Joseph took the jewelry box from his father and stared down at the rings, transfixed. He remembered how they used to gleam on his mother's hand. She had been a smart, strong woman, and a strict, but loving, mother. Sonia reminded him of her in some ways. He would be proud to present her with these rings. Unshed tears tried to clog his throat. He cleared it. "Thank you, father. I am honored."

"I have always considered you my successor. Your brother's shortcomings were apparent to me early on. You were always the focused one -- the smart one," Dwe said.

"I promise to make you proud, Father."

"You already have, my son," Dwe said. He gave Joseph a hug.

Joseph never felt closer to his father than he did at that moment.

Chapter VII

A few months later, Sonia and Joseph sat at a table in a formal French restaurant. They had just finished a lovely, romantic meal. The waiter cleared away their plates and brought in two small covered trays.

Sonia looked at Joseph and smiled. What was this? She hadn't ordered dessert. It was just like him to take the reins and surprise her this way. She eyed the tray covers wondering what delectable treats lay underneath them.

The waiter set one covered tray in front of Sonia and the other in front of Joseph. He left briefly, then returned with a cart containing two champagne flutes and a bottle of champagne nestled inside an ice bucket. He placed the flutes onto the table. With much flourish, he popped the cork on the champagne and poured the golden elixir into the flutes. "Enjoy your dessert."

"Thank you," Joseph said.

Sonia raised her eyebrows. Joseph was certainly going all out tonight. What was the occasion? Was it their half-year anniversary or something? She'd never put much stock in such things. She'd always been more practical than romantic. Had she missed it? No. They'd just started dating five months ago.

In the time since they'd returned from the trip to Liberia, she'd discovered things about Joseph she'd never known before. Either that or he had changed a lot since they dated back in college. Sure, he was still the most sexually dominant man she'd ever been with, and the most exciting. She felt the warmth of a blush rise in her cheeks as she thought about the things he liked to do to her -- in and out of bed -- and how much they turned her on. Who knew that she'd enjoy being ordered to strip, flipped like a pancake, spanked? And the way he looked at her, – with such hunger. She bit her lip.

But there was more to the man. He also had a tender side – a romantic one. The same man who demanded that she give him anything and everything in the bedroom often surprised her with flowers for no reason, held open doors for her, called her "my lady" and loved to cuddle and hold hands. The combination made her feel both wanted and cherished.

She looked up to find him watching her, a half smile on his handsome face. He did that a lot. She would wake up sometimes and find him looking at her just like that. She smiled back at him. "I didn't know you had ordered dessert. You ordered champagne, too. So, what are we celebrating?"

Joseph reached across the table, uncovered Sonia's tray and revealed the jewelry box sitting underneath. He picked it up, rose from his chair, got down on one knee next to her, and opened it.

Sonia's mind went blank for a moment. Then it hit her. He was going to propose. She couldn't believe it. She stared down at the ring and then at him in open-mouthed astonishment.

"Sonia, I love you more than life. I have ever since I first saw you in that campus nightclub so many years ago, and I'll never stop loving you. I want to spend the rest of my life with you, to grow old with you, to have children with you. Will you marry me?" he asked.

She didn't need to think about it. She'd never been happier than she'd been the past few months. The thought of spending the rest of her life with this man brought her nothing but joy. Tears of happiness pricked at her eyes and clogged her throat. She cleared it and nodded. "Yes. Yes Joseph, I'll marry you."

Joseph beamed. He drew the engagement ring from the box, took Sonia's left hand and slipped it onto her finger. It was a perfect fit.

Sonia leaned forward and kissed Joseph.

Nearby restaurant patrons who had witnessed the scene applauded. Sonia barely heard them.

***

Ten months later, Sonia lay in bed, drifting between being awake and being asleep. Joseph entered their bedroom. "Wake up, my lady. I made you breakfast."

"Hmmm?" Sonia sat up and rubbed her eyes.

"Where do you want the tray?" he asked.

"Tray?" She stopped rubbing her eyes and looked up. Joseph was standing there holding a tray of food. "You made me breakfast? How sweet! Set it down right here next to me." She patted the mattress.

"Yes, my lady." Joseph set the tray down. "I made you toast, scrambled eggs, and a little fruit salad. Here, taste." He filled the fork with scrambled egg and brought it toward her mouth.

As the eggs drew closer to her nostrils, Sonia got a whiff and felt nausea swiftly overtake her. She clapped her hand to her mouth, jumped out of the bed and ran into the bathroom. She came out a few minutes later feeling weak. She climbed back onto the bed. The tray was still there. She looked down at the food and felt her empty stomach heave. She willed herself not to throw up again.

"Oh honey," she said, "I don't know what's wrong with me. I feel so nauseous. I'm sorry. I can't eat the beautiful breakfast you fixed me."

"Don't be silly," Joseph said. "Are you all right? Do you have a fever?" He placed a hand on her brow. "You should go see your doctor right away."

Sonia shook her head. "I don't need a doctor. It's probably just a migraine coming on or something. I get those sometimes."

"Get back under the covers." Joseph's tone brooked no argument. "I'll take the tray away and bring you some ginger tea instead."

"No, really. I'll be all right. I have to get ready for work."

"Nonsense. Work can wait. Call your assistant and have her cancel your appointments for today. If you feel better later, then maybe you can go in this afternoon," he said.

"Come on Joseph. Aren't you overreacting just a little bit?" she asked.

"Didn't you just get sick in the bathroom?" He pointed a finger at her. "And don't lie to me -- I heard you."

Sonia winced. He had her there. "Okay, okay. I'll call my assistant."

Joseph handed her the telephone, picked up the breakfast tray and left the bedroom.

Sonia dialed her office. Suzette picked up on the first ring. "Sonia Johnson's office."

"Hi Suzette. It's me. I woke up completely nauseous. I don't know what's wrong with me. It's probably a migraine, but my head isn't killing me and I don't see any of those little flashing lights I usually see when I get a migraine. I'm just so nauseous. Anyway, my husband ordered me to stay in bed this morning and see how I feel later," Sonia said.

Suzette laughed. "Your husband ordered you to stay in bed and you really are? Wow. I never thought I'd see the day. You must really feel awful. Nauseous, huh? Are you sure it's not morning sickness?"

"Morning sickness? Why would I have morning sickness? Don't pregnant women get that? I'm not pregnant," Sonia said.

"Are you sure?" Suzette asked.

Sonia tried to remember the last time she'd gotten her period. She frowned. Try as she might, she couldn't remember. Her heartbeat increased and she sat up straighter in the bed. "Oh my God. I better pick up a pregnancy test at the drug store."

"Yeah. You do that. In the meantime, I'll cancel your appointments for today. Take the day off. You work too hard, anyway," Suzette said.

"Yeah right. What's on my schedule for today?" Sonia asked.

"You just have a meeting with your associate mentee and a shareholders meeting. We can reschedule the meeting with your mentee for tomorrow," Suzette said.

"Okay. I'll see you this afternoon. I'll be reading and responding to my e-mails and you can transfer any calls to my cell phone. I'll pick up," Sonia said.

"Okay. Feel better and get one of those tests," she said.

An hour later, Joseph and Sonia sat on the bed. Joseph had his arms around her and she leaned back against him, feeling nervous and tense.

"Will you relax? I will be happy either way," he said. He wrapped his arms tighter around her.

Maybe he would. But how did she feel about it? On one hand, having a child with Joseph would be a beautiful thing. He'd make a great father and the child would never want for anything. On the other hand, she didn't know if she was ready for such a huge responsibility. What kind of mother would she make? Children weren't really part of her life plan. She was a career woman. She'd always thought she'd have a child if whoever she married really wanted one, but she'd never felt the urge to reproduce herself. Having a kid would definitely change their lives and she was happy the way things were.

"I just never thought I'd get pregnant so quickly," she said. "I thought we'd enjoy each other for a couple of years before we decided to have children. I'm a little nervous about it. I mean, what kind of mother will I be?"

"You worry too much. You will be a wonderful mother. I knew that when I asked you to marry me. You have a wonderful way with children. Look how your best friends' children adore you," he said.

"Yeah, but it's different when they're your kids and you have them all the time" she said.

"Is it time to look yet?" he asked.

"Yes. I guess I better go look," she said.

Joseph squeezed her close, kissed her on the cheek and then let her go. She rose and headed into the master bathroom. She looked at the test stick and gasped. It was positive. The little plus sign was there clear as day. She stood there for a moment, staring at it.

What was she going to do? She wasn't ready to have a child yet. She closed her eyes, opened them and looked at the test again. The little plus sign was still there, just mocking her. Ready or not, a little baby was on the way. She'd have to get ready.

She took a deep breath, blew it out and re-entered the bedroom. "Alright Daddy, when this kid gets up at three o'clock in the morning looking for a bottle, I'm waking you up to feed him. And you had better not complain."

Joseph's eyes lit up. He smiled broadly, jumped off the bed, grabbed Sonia in a bear hug, and spun her around and around. He set her down and kissed her soundly. "Yes! I am going to be a father! You have made me the happiest man in the world. I love you. I love you. I love you." He punctuated each declaration of love with a kiss.

Sonia laughed. "Well, I think you had a little something to do with it too. Did you even hear what I said about you getting up in the middle of the night to feed the brat? I was serious."

"I don't care," he said. "I'll get up happily to feed my son."

"Yeah, but what if it's a girl?" she asked. "You'd better get up and feed her too."

Joseph pulled Sonia to him and kissed her again, this time long and slow. She felt the heat began to stir in her belly. He broke off the kiss and looked down at her.

"If she is half as beautiful as her mama, she will wrap me around her little finger," he said. He led her back to bed.

**

Eight months later, Sonia sat in a hospital bed in a private room holding her newborn son. She stared down at his little face and felt a wave of love so powerful it shook her.

He was so tiny, so perfect. She wondered how she could feel so exhausted and so exhilarated at the same time.

Dwe, her parents and Joseph surrounded the bed and admired him.

"Oh, just look at him. Isn't he just the cutest little thing?" her mom asked. She put her forefinger into his little hand and smiled when he squeezed a tiny fist around it.

"My grandson is quite handsome," her father said, preening as if he had arranged the whole thing himself.

"My grandson will grow up to be a king one day," Dwe said.

Sonia smiled and shook her head. "Come on people. You'll just have to share him."

"Have you picked a name for him yet?" her mom asked.

"Yes. We've decided to name him David Dwe Saytumah in honor of his two grandfathers," Sonia said.

"I am honored," Dwe said. "Thank you." A single tear slid down the old man's cheek.

"After all we did for the girl, it was the least she could do," Senator Johnson said.

Sonia's mother frowned at her husband. "David! What a thing to say."

The senator grinned and looked down at Sonia. "Just kidding. You've made me very happy, sweetheart. I'm so proud of you." He leaned down and pressed a kiss to her brow.

Sonia could feel her eyes well up. "Oh Daddy, you'll make me cry."

The duty nurse entered the room. "Okay. Visiting hours are over. Mama needs to rest and this little tyke needs to eat. He's been through a lot today. You can come back tomorrow."

Dwe and Sonia's parents kissed them goodbye and left. Joseph sat on the side of the bed while Sonia breastfed their son. He gazed down at them. "A son. Words cannot express the joy you've brought me, my love." He leaned down and planted a tender kiss on her lips.

Sonia smiled at him and then at the little creature suckling at her breast. She'd never felt so content in her whole life.

Chapter VIII

Sonia lifted a lid off one of the pots bubbling in front of her and stirred its fragrant contents. She replaced the lid then paused and glanced at the baby monitor on the kitchen counter. She thought she'd heard David waking up early from his nap. Thankfully, the monitor remained silent. She picked up a knife and began chopping vegetables.

Joseph walked into the kitchen. She threw him a smile. "Hi honey. David's taking a nap so I thought I'd take advantage and make us a home-cooked meal for dinner."

When Joseph didn't reply, she turned to look at him. He was just standing there staring into space. She put the knife down, wiped her hands on a kitchen towel and went to him. "Honey, what's wrong? Are you all right?"

"It's my father. He died early this morning," he said.

"Died? What do you mean died? What did he die of?" she asked.

"Cancer. They said he had cancer," Joseph said. His voice broke. "He never told me. I can't believe it."

Sonia stepped in and put her arms around him. "Oh baby, I'm so sorry."

He buried his head in her neck and cried. She held on tight until he was finished, then sat him down at the kitchen table and brought him a box of tissues. "Who's making the arrangements?"

He wiped his face with his hands, then grabbed some tissues and blew his nose. "Saye will do that, with help from Fatima. The funeral will be held in Liberia."

Sonia stifled a groan. Of course the funeral would take place in Liberia. She felt torn. On one hand, she wanted to be there for him. On the other hand, she needed to be with their son. He was only two months old.

"Will you go alone or do you want me to come with you?" she asked.

"I want you and David with me," he said.

"Is it safe enough for him there? I mean, he's so little," she said.

"Of course it's safe enough for him. We will arrange for a nanny to take care of him while we attend the funeral and make other public appearances," he said.

"A nanny? Who? I mean, I have to meet and approve her before I leave her with our newborn son," Sonia said.

When Joseph looked up at her, his red-rimmed eyes ready for battle, she realized that maybe she needed to be a little more accommodating. She raised her hands in front of her palms facing outward. "Let's not argue about this now. I'll just interview this nanny when we get there and then, if I like her, I'll see how she is with David. If I don't like her, I'll just keep David with me wherever we go and we'll just have to keep my public appearances to a minimum."

"Fair enough." He stood up and reached for her. She went into his arms. He rested his forehead onto hers. "What would I do without you?"

***

Two days later, Sonia and Joseph stood in the living room of the Saytumah family mansion with all of the guests who had attended the funeral. Everyone milled about, talking quietly. Servants in uniforms with black ribbons tied around their right arms threaded among them carrying trays of hors d'oeuvres. Tyrone and Tara walked up to them.

"Joseph, I'm so sorry for your loss. Your father was a great man," Tyrone said.

"Thank you," Joseph said.

"Although I wish you were visiting on a happier occasion, I hope that you and Sonia will have the opportunity to come by and see us before you go back to America," Tara said.

"We will see. There is a lot to be done before we go. The will is being read tonight and my brother and I have some arrangements to make," Joseph said.

"Of course. Have you made any plans yet with respect to the company?" Tyrone asked.

"No. That's one of the things we are going to have to deal with. I still can't believe he's gone," Joseph said.

Tara put a hand on his arm. "If you need anything, you know that we're here for you."

"Thank you," Joseph said.

President Sirleaf and one of her aides walked up to Joseph and Sonia. "Joseph," she said, "I am so sorry for your loss."

"Thank you for your kind words at the funeral, Madame President, and for making sure that my father received full honors," Joseph said.

"The country lost a great man when your father died. Speaking of that, Joseph, I now have an opening in the Liberian ministry that needs to be filled. Your father was doing a wonderful job for Liberia. It will take a very special person to fill his place. I know that he always considered you to be his successor. That is why I am asking you to fill out his term," she said.

"Fill out his term? " Joseph asked. "You mean here in Liberia?"

"Yes," President Sirleaf said.

"I am honored Madame President. Obviously, I will have to discuss this with my wife," Joseph said.

"Of course. I would expect no less. You have a week to decide. I hope you will take this opportunity to serve your country. We need all the help we can get in rebuilding the damage done by the civil war," she said.

"Yes. I know. No matter where I am, Liberia is always in my heart. I will let you know my decision," Joseph said.

"Madame President, we have another engagement we have to get to this afternoon," the president's aide said.

The president nodded, then turned back to Joseph and Sonia. "Well, we have to go now, but not before I congratulate you both on the birth of your son," she said.

"Thank you, Madame President," Sonia said. "I've been following your administration in the news. As a woman, it fills me with pride to see the progress you've made here."

The president smiled. "Thank you. I hear that you are an attorney in your country and a very good one at that. It is my hope that, if Joseph decides to come to Liberia and finish out his father's term, you too will lend your expertise to my administration," she said.

"We will certainly consider your request," Sonia said.

***

After the funeral, Sonia and Joseph returned to Joseph's room. Joseph took off his suit and hung it in the closet. Sonia had gone into the restroom to remove her makeup.

She'd been quiet ever since their conversation with the president. He could almost see the wheels turning in her mind. He knew the night would not end before they discussed the president's request.

Joseph could not believe his luck when she had asked him to finish out his father's term. He couldn't have planned a better way to continue his father's work. The Ministry position would put him close to the president and give him control over the Liberian military forces. Once he gained the president's trust and control of the military, he'd be able to put his plan into motion. Liberia would be his for the taking.

He turned to look at the door of the restroom and frowned. Everything else was falling into place. Sonia was the only uncertain factor. He needed to get her on board. It was imperative that she agree to allow him to finish out his father's term and that she and their son joined him in Liberia. Having them there and having Sonia assist the president would serve to deepen the president's trust in him. Sonia's background would also serve to strengthen the historical ties between America and Liberia both before and after he carried out his plan. His father had been a very wise man. He had known, from the moment Joseph told him about Sonia all those years ago, that she would prove to be an invaluable asset.

But it ran much deeper than that for him. He needed her and their son. He needed their love and support. Sonia had been a rock this past week. Her unwavering support and his son's blind trust were the only things that got him through the shock and grief caused by his father's unexpected death. He needed them by his side. It was that simple.

Sonia padded into the bedroom wearing slippers and a silk robe. Joseph looked at her naked face. She'd never looked more beautiful to him. She headed into the closet. After a moment, she emerged and took a seat on the bed. "So, are you really considering accepting the president's offer to finish out your father's term?" she asked.

"Yes. It would be a great honor to serve my country. It is what my father would have wanted."

"How long is the rest of your father's term?" she asked.

"He would have been up for re-election in about two years," he said.

Sonia's eyes widened. "Two years? What about our lives in the U.S.? What about my family? My job? How can we just take off like that for two whole years?"

"You are already on maternity leave. Couldn't you take a sabbatical or something?" he asked.

"Well, I've heard about other attorneys taking a year off to do different types of public service work. I guess this would kind of fit into that category," she said.

Aha. He knew his wife. The fact that she had come up with a precedent for taking the time off from work told him that she had seriously considered President Sirleaf's offer and thought about how to make it work. There was hope after all.

"Yes it would. You could tell your firm that you want to take a sabbatical to perform public service for your husband's country. You could even apply for a grant with an American organization to sponsor the work you would be doing for the Liberian government to make it more legitimate from your firm's perspective. But it's not as if we need the money or anything. My father was a very wealthy man. With my inheritance, you never have to work another day in your life," he said.

Sonia twisted her lips. "Joseph, you know it's not just about the money with me. I have a profession – not a hobby. I'd lose my mind being a housewife."

Joseph chuckled. "I know. And you would be terrible at it, my lady."

Sonia's mouth fell open. She gasped then grabbed one of the bed pillows and chucked it at his head. He ducked. She laughed.

Then she sobered and looked lost in thought.

He walked up to her, pulled her to her feet and put his arms around her. Her muscles were rigid – tense. He reached under her chin, lifted it and looked into her eyes. "If the president of the United States asked you to take a position in his cabinet, would you decline – even though it would mean leaving New York and moving to Washington, D.C.? Wouldn't you want to have me and our son by your side? Wouldn't you expect for me to accept that? This is no different."

She leaned back a little and stabbed a finger into his chest. "It is different and you know it. Washington D.C. is not Liberia."

"It might as well be. I would still have to leave my job at the Liberian consulate and be away from my friends in New York."

"What about my family?" she asked.

Joseph shrugged. "You could fly back and visit them from time to time and they could visit us here. It's not like we see them all the time when we are in New York."

"True. But my mother will not be happy if we decide to do this. She'll worry about us with all of the unrest here. And both my folks will miss playing with their grandson. What about the baby? Will he be safe here?" Sonia asked.

There it was. He knew that Sonia's concern for their son's well-being would be the most important factor in her decision whether to come to Liberia. "Has he suffered any ill effects since we've been here?"

"No. But we've only been here a couple of days. On the other hand, I have to admit that the nanny Saye and Fatima hired appears to be working out pretty well. I like her. More importantly, David took to her right away. She's good with him," Sonia said.

"Saye and I grew up here and we managed to survive. We are only talking about two years, Sonia. After that, we will see," Joseph said.

Sonia sent him a stern look. "What do you mean we will see? I couldn't possibly spend more time than that here. I have a life to get back to in the U.S."

Joseph kissed her. "Stop worrying. Everything is going to be fine. With you and my son by my side, we can't lose. Come on, honey. I really need to do this, and I can't do it without you."

He felt her muscles relax and stifled a triumphant smile. He had convinced her.

"Okay," she said, "but only for two years. After that, I get my life back. Deal?"

"This is part of your life too. You belong at my side," he said.

She jabbed her finger into his chest again and looked up at him. He winced at the tiny pain and the serious look in her eyes. "Do we have a deal, mister?"

Joseph crossed his fingers behind her back and nodded his head. "Yes my lady. We have a deal."

***

A few weeks later, Sonia sat on the couch with her mother in her parents' living room. Her father played with David. She'd dreaded telling them about her decision to go to Liberia with Joseph, but she couldn't put it off any longer.

"So, we'd just be moving to Liberia for two years. We'll come back to the U.S. a couple of times each year to visit with you, and you could come visit us too," she said.

"Liberia? Is it even safe there?" Her mother wrung her hands. "They've been reporting on the news about pockets of unrest there. You're going to put yourself into that sort of danger? What about my grandson?"

"Ma, the house is very well guarded. And Saye and Fatima hired this great nanny to help me take care of David. He did really well there the last time we visited," Sonia said.

"But what about your job, your friends, your life here in the U.S.?"

"Part of my life is being with my husband. This is a great honor for him and David and I should be by his side. I've already asked my firm for permission to take a sabbatical and they've agreed. Other lawyers at the firm have taken sabbaticals to do public service, take political positions, and things like that. The firm was pretty open to the idea," Sonia said.

"But what will you do while you're there? You'll go crazy sitting there in the mansion for two years while your husband helps to run the government of Liberia," her mother said.

"Well, Joseph and I have friends there -- Tyrone and Tara Nkrumah. You met them at the wedding. Plus, President Sirleaf requested my help in negotiating business deals for the Liberian government. It's also a great opportunity for me to explore my interest in writing. I've always wanted to write a book. Plus, I'll get to spend more time with David. That's something I couldn't do if I were here working all the time," Sonia said.

"You seem to given this a great deal of thought," her father said.

"I have, Daddy," Sonia said.

"Well, if it's something you really want to do and you've thought it through, then we shouldn't stand in your way. We're going to miss you and my little buddy here an awful lot though. And we're going to worry about you both," he said.

"Yes, we are. I don't think this is a good idea at all. Are you sure he isn't forcing you to do something you don't want to do?" her mother asked.

Sonia rolled her eyes. Why did her mother always have to act as if she couldn't make a single good decision for herself? "Of course not, Ma. This is something we've decided to do as a family."

"Okay. Okay. Since you're dead set on going, I can't stop you. But I don't like it." Her mother folded her arms and rubbed them with her hands. "I don't have a good feeling about this at all."

Her mother's words sent a strange feeling of foreboding through Sonia. Her mother's "feelings" had proven accurate time and time again over the years. Like the time her father travelled to Israel and the American embassy was bombed. Her mother seemed to have a sort of sixth sense about these things.

She wondered, for the tenth time, whether she'd made the right decision. But it was too late to turn back now. Joseph had already accepted the position and she'd already taken the sabbatical from work and shipped the majority of her and David's clothes and other necessary items ahead. For better or worse, they were going to Liberia. She'd just have to make it work.

Chapter IX

A year later, Sonia sat in the living room of the Saytumah family mansion, paging through an American magazine.

Fatima walked into the room. "Are you okay, Mrs. Saytumah? Can I get you anything?"

"Please, call me Sonia. I'm okay," Sonia sighed. "I guess I'm just a little bored.

"Where is David?" Fatima asked.

"The nanny has him. Do you have time to come sit with me for a while?" Sonia asked.

"Of course, Mrs. Saytumah. I mean Sonia." Fatima joined her on the couch.

"So, how has working with Joseph been for you? Is it very different from working with Dwe?" Sonia asked.

"Well, my duties are still the same. But Joseph is much more even tempered than his father was. That is not to say that I did not enjoy working with Mr. Saytumah, but he could be a little unpredictable at times." Fatima covered her mouth with one hand. "Oh, but I should not say such things."

"Nonsense," Sonia said. "I'm the one who asked. Joseph has certainly been busy lately. I don't think I've seen him for more than five minutes since they swore him into his new position."

"Yes. We have been very busy. There is much work to be done in rebuilding Liberia," Fatima said.

"I know. And I don't mean to be selfish or whiny, but I guess I thought it would be a little different -- that I'd be playing more of a role. The last time we were here, the President requested my assistance in negotiating business deals for Liberia. Although I've gotten to do some of that, it's not exactly steady work. As a partner in a corporate law firm, I'm used to having a lot more to do on a daily basis. It's a little hard for me to just lie back and do nothing.

Fatima raised her eyebrows. "Many women would kill for the opportunity to relax and enjoy their home and their children. To not have to work so hard just to survive."

"I know. I know. I shouldn't complain. It's just that, at times like this, when David isn't here, I sort of miss my old life," Sonia said. "What do the other ministers' wives do to stay busy?"

Fatima shrugged. "Some of them just sit back and enjoy their position. They stay home and tend to their children, plan parties and other social events, and shop. A few of them do volunteer work."

"Volunteer work? What sort of volunteer work?" Sonia asked.

"One of the ministers' wives volunteers at a rape crisis center. You met her at the installation ceremony – Mrs. Dagher," Fatima said.

An image of a beautiful, dark-skinned statuesque woman appeared in Sonia's mind and made her smile. She had liked Mrs. Dagher. She was friendly and had a wicked sense of humor. The idea of doing volunteer work appealed to Sonia. She'd have to give her a call and set up a lunch date with her.

"Can you get me her number?" Sonia asked.

"Yes, ma'am. I'll get that for you right away," Fatima said.

"Thank you, Fatima. And thanks for sitting with me and listening to me rant. I'm sure you have tons of work to do," Sonia said

"It was my pleasure. Call me if you need anything else," Fatima said.

"Thanks. I will," Sonia said.

***

A month later, Sonia and Tara hung out in the Nkrumah mansion's family room.

"So, how have you been?" Tara asked.

"I've been good. I've been volunteering a lot lately at the rape crisis center. That work can really tear your guts out. It's unbelievable what some of those girls have been through and what they're still dealing with. But it's given me something meaningful to do, which I really needed. Joseph has been missing in action since we got here. He's been so busy, I feel like I only see him at night for quickies in the dark and at social functions," Sonia said.

Tara laughed. "Well, at least you're still having sex. I've heard some of the ministers' wives complain they don't even get that. Although I suspect their husbands are getting those needs attended elsewhere."

Sonia chuckled. "Not Joseph. He comes home to get what he wants."

Tara fanned herself. "Sounds hot. Now why can't I find a man like that?"

Sonia reached over and patted Tara's arm. "You will, girlie. You will."

The news came on the radio. They listened to the announcer talk about pockets of unrest in the countryside. Sonia frowned. She had noticed that security around the mansion and the rape crisis center seemed to be tighter – more noticeable.

"I'm a little worried about all of this unrest in the countryside. Are we safe?" Sonia asked.

"Well, in Liberia, 'safe' is a relative term. But you are protected in the Saytumah family compound and here. And, so far, the unrest has only been in the countryside -- not in Monrovia. If you were in danger, Joseph would be among the first to know. I'm sure he would send you and David out of the country," Tara said.

"But what about him? He's not invincible," Sonia said.

"Well, you know how men are. He would stay and fight for his country. He would feel it was his duty," Tara said.

A servant ran into the room. He spoke quickly in a thick Liberian accent and waved his arms around -- clearly agitated about something. Tyrone and Tara turned to look at Sonia with grim expressions on their faces.

Sonia felt a chill go down her spine. "What? What's happened? I couldn't make out much of what he said."

"There's been a coup. Rebels have taken over the Presidential mansion. They escorted the president to the airport and sent her into exile at gunpoint," Tyrone said.

Sonia couldn't believe her ears. The very thing she feared the most seemed to be happening. Her throat tightened. "A coup? Oh my God. I've to get back to the mansion. I have to get to my son. Joseph -- oh my God. Is he okay? Where is he?"

"At the Presidential mansion, I imagine," Tara said drily. "Joseph is doing just fine. He's the one who executed the coup."

Sonia drew her brows together. No. She couldn't have heard that right. "What? No. That can't possibly be true. What are you talking about?"

"Sonia, it was Joseph who led the rebels that took over the Presidential mansion. Did you know about this? How long has he been planning this?" Tyrone asked.

It was Joseph who had done this? No. Hell no. That had to be wrong. She shook her head, grabbed her purse from the coffee table and rose from her seat. "No. There must be some sort of mistake. I have to get back to the house." She turned toward the door, but Tara stood up and grabbed her arm, stopping her.

"Wait a minute," Tara said. "You can't leave yet. We don't know if it's safe out there."

Fury and frustration rose swiftly within Sonia. She whirled on Tara so quickly that the woman released her arm and took a step back. Sonia narrowed her eyes and stabbed a finger in Tara's direction. "No! You wait a minute. I don't know what the hell you people are talking about and I'm not wasting another second trying to figure it out. I have to go see if my husband and my son are okay and you can't stop me." With that, she stalked out of the living room and out the front door.

"Sonia!" Tara called after her.

Sonia kept going. She walked up to the limousine parked outside, got in and ordered the driver to take her home.

The streets of Monrovia were in pandemonium. Although there were always throngs of people walking the streets -- especially in the downtown area -- the number of people milling about had tripled. Some were celebrating, others protesting. Traffic was almost at a standstill.

At one point, they passed through such an angry mob that Sonia feared for their lives. Men ran up to the limousine and started pounding on it with their fists. The driver pulled his gun out, thumbed off the safety and laid the weapon on the seat next to him. The men backed off.

***

When she got back to the Saytumah family mansion, the first thing Sonia did was track down the nanny and check on David. He was playing with his toys in the nursery -- happy as could be. She picked him up and held him tight, finally releasing the breath she didn't even know she'd been holding. She closed her eyes as relief flooded through her body and some of the tension eased. *He's safe. Thank you God.*

Not wanting to let him go, she walked over to the rocking chair and sat down. At first, David squirmed restlessly. But, when she picked up a book from the table and began reading to him, he snuggled up to her and let her rock him to sleep. She put David down for a nap under the watchful eye of the nanny and then went in search of her husband. But he wasn't home.

She paced back and forth in the living room waiting for Joseph. All kinds of thoughts and horrible scenarios ran through her mind. Where was he? Was he dead? Lying in a ditch? Had he been taken prisoner?

An hour later, he walked into the room. Sonia ran into his arms and burrowed her head in his chest. He held her while the words came flooding out of her mouth. "Joseph! Oh my God. Are you okay? What the hell is going on? I was at Tara and Tyrone's house when a servant ran in and told us there had been a coup. They said the Presidential mansion had been taken over by rebels and that you were leading the coup! Oh baby, I was so scared. I knew there had to be some mistake."

Hearing nothing but silence, she pushed back a little and looked up at him. Something was wrong. "It was a mistake, wasn't it?"

He looked back at her, a hesitant expression on his face. He took her by the hands and led her over to the couch. "Sonia, come sit with me."

Sonia let him draw her down onto the couch. He sat down next to her and continued to hold her hands in his. "There was a coup. But you do not have to worry, my lady. We are safe."

"What do you mean, 'we are safe'? If there was a coup, how could we be safe?" She didn't understand. Then it hit her. She snatched her hands out from his, jumped up off the couch and turned to fully face him. "So it is true. You were the one who executed the coup. Why Joseph? Why did you do this?"

"There was growing unrest in Liberia. President Sirleaf made a lot of progress since she came in, but we Liberians are an impatient people and it was not happening fast enough. Poverty in this country is tremendous. We still do not have running water or electricity in parts of the countryside. Unemployment is still over fifty percent. President Sirleaf wanted to maintain a democratic system. The Liberian army was getting restless as were the people. It was only a matter of time before someone else staged a coup. Liberians need a firm hand. I thought that, if I executed a coup, at least I could make sure President Sirleaf left the country alive. I did it for Liberia, and to protect her safety," he said.

"But what about us? What about your son? You put us all in danger by doing this. What did you think we would do, stay in Liberia and live happily ever after? What about my life back in New York? Did you even think about that before you went and executed a coup? Now that you're president of Liberia, what are we supposed to do?" Sonia asked.

"Your life is here with me. By my side. You and David belong here. David is a Liberian by blood. You are my wife," he said.

"What?" Sonia stared at him, not quite believing the words that were coming out of his mouth or the utterly resolute and matter-of-fact tone with which he said them. Then she looked into his eyes and she knew. The mask was gone and she saw, for the first time, who her husband really was -- a manipulative, conniving, megalomaniac.

"You bastard," she said. "You planned this all along, didn't you? You never intended for us to go back to New York." Her voice broke and she shook with fury. "You planned to take over the country from the very beginning, didn't you?"

When he just sat there, staring at her, she became even more enraged. She threw her hands up and began to pace back and forth. "Well, I don't care what you do. I'm going back to New York. To hell with you. You can stay here and run your country and do whatever the hell you want to do. I'm taking my son back to safety and to his grandparents who must be going crazy with worry right now."

Joseph rose from the couch and glowered at her. "You can do whatever you want, but you are not taking my son with you." His voice was dangerously quiet.

Sonia stopped pacing and stared at him, her heart constricting in her chest. "What? What do you mean?"

"David is not leaving the country. If you want to be with him, you will have to stay here with me," he said.

"You would keep my son from me? What gives you the fucking right to do that when it was me who gave birth to him, me who breast-fed him, me woke up in the middle of the night with him? What gives you that right?"

"I am the president of Liberia. I can do whatever I want to, and you had better start thinking about that," he said.

Sonia saw red. "You fucking bastard! I hate you!" She flew at him and tried her level best to claw his eyes out.

Joseph grabbed her by the wrists and pushed her backward. Hard. She landed on her behind on the rug. Dazed, she looked up at him, breathing heavily. He stared down at her for a moment, then stalked out of the room. She stared after him in disbelief.

This couldn't be happening. Who was that man and what had he done with her husband? It had all been a lie -- their marriage, the life they'd built together. The man she loved, the man she thought she had married, didn't exist. It all had been a lie.

She lay there on the floor and cried -- the sobs racking her body, the pain of his deception and betrayal so intense she thought she would die.

When she had no tears left, she wiped her face and headed to the nursery. David was sleeping peacefully – blissfully unaware of the havoc taking place around him. She crawled into bed with him.

***

Back at the Nkrumah family mansion, Tyrone and Tara sat in the situation room reporting the recent events to their handler.

"We have now received verification that Joseph Saytumah has executed a coup and taken over the Presidential mansion," Tara said.

"What is the status of President Sirleaf?" Ben asked.

"She is alive. Joseph had her escorted to the airport and put on a plane bound for London," Tyrone said.

Ben sighed. "That's a relief. How did this happen? Your assignment was to keep this from happening."

"Well sir, we didn't expect for Joseph to pick up where his father left off in terms of the coup. We expected for him to carry on with the arms business since he ran it for his father prior to his death, but it was much more likely for Saye to try to execute a coup. We did not believe that Joseph and Saye had amassed enough political power yet to pull it off. Joseph just took over his father's position a few months ago. We just didn't see this happening for at least another year," Tara said.

"There have been too many mistakes made on this mission. We need to move, and move fast, before Joseph is able to legitimize his new government. The world might have recognized Saye for the brutal dictator he would become, but Joseph is much more polished than his brother. With his wife's political connections and the passage of time, he might just be able to smooth this over in the international arena. We need someone on the inside to help us get the leverage we need. What about Sonia Saytumah? Do you think you'll be able to turn her into an asset?" Ben asked.

"Either she's an Academy-Award caliber actress or she was genuinely shocked to learn that Joseph had carried out a coup," Tyrone said.

Tara shook her head. "No-one's that good of an actress. She was terrified and very worried about Joseph. I don't think she believed us when we told her it was him who had executed the coup. With that being said, we still don't know how she'll react when she finds out it's true. She could accept it and decide to help him or she could reject it, and then who knows how Joseph will react. I believe they really have feelings for each other; still, that won't stop him from carrying out his mission."

"Well, we need someone on the inside and it sounds like Sonia has Joseph's trust. He won't expect for her to ally with us and double-cross him. I want you to feel her out and figure out the best approach. Should we appeal to her patriotic side or lean on her by threatening criminal prosecution? We also need to find out how much she knows. She may be less likely to remain loyal to him if she knows the whole truth," Ben said.

"But Ben, Sonia is a civilian. We sent a trained agent in and he was killed. How can we expect Sonia to be able to pull this off?" Tara asked.

"Women have been sneaking around and lying to men for centuries. It's called marriage," Tyrone said.

Tara rolled her eyes at him.

"Tara, if you have reservations about continuing this mission, let me know now. Otherwise, I want you to devise a plan to make this work," Ben said.

Tara swallowed the rest of her protests. She wanted to see the mission through to the end. "I have no reservations, sir. We'll get to work on that plan right away."

"Good," Ben said. "I expect to receive weekly progress reports." He signed off.

Tara sat back in her chair and blew out a breath.

Tyrone raised his eyebrows. "That was a little tense."

"You don't say," Tara said.

"Look, I know how you feel about using a civilian to get what we need -- especially a sweet one like Sonia. I have reservations about that myself. But, as much as I hate to admit it, Ben's right. It's our only play," Tyrone said.

"Don't you think I know that?" Tara said. She sighed. "I'm sorry. I shouldn't be snapping at you. It's just that I don't know what I'll do if she ends up getting killed and that poor little boy is left without a mother."

"Well then, I guess we'd better make sure that doesn't happen," he said.

Tara nodded. "Yup. Let's get to work."

Chapter X

Sonia sat in the family room of the Presidential mansion. Her son played with his toys on the floor. Sonia watched him thoughtfully.

A lot had changed. It felt as if the coup had taken place two years ago instead of two months ago. Joseph had the servants pack up their things and move them into the Presidential mansion within days of the coup. They were escorted by soldiers who kept guard outside. Sonia had felt like an intruder invading what had just been President Sirleaf's home. She still felt that way.

On top of that, the place was huge. There were not only living quarters, but a huge hall and salons for entertaining, and several offices. It was a maze Sonia would have to learn her way around if she didn't want to keep getting lost on the way to the makeshift nursery they'd created for David.

President Sirleaf had had an army of servants, staff members, and armed guards to tend to her every need. They'd inherited that staff. Although Sonia was surrounded by dozens of people at all times and had virtually no privacy, she'd never felt so alone or so afraid. Although the staff members were careful not to show a hint of emotion, Sonia could only imagine what they felt about their president being taken away at gunpoint. Neither she nor David would ever be safe in this place. She hugged herself and rubbed her arms.

Whatever love she had felt for her husband had died the night she found out who he truly was. At first, he'd tried to act as if nothing had changed between them. When he entered their bedroom a few nights after the coup and tried to have sex with her, she felt nothing but revulsion. She fought him and continued to fight him until he stopped making advances and retreated to his side of the bed. She'd lain there, wide awake, not trusting him to leave her alone while she slept. Finally, at dawn, he got up, took a shower, dressed and left.

Later that day, he'd sat her down in the family room and lectured her about her duties as the first lady of Liberia. She was to conduct herself as a lady, attend and plan social events and political functions, oversee the redecoration of the Presidential mansion, and use her charm, legal skills, and negotiation skills to assist his administration. She also was expected to perform her wifely duties.

When Sonia laughed out loud at that last bit, he threw her a very serious look. "I understand that you are upset right now. It's only natural. You have suffered quite a shock," he had said. "In light of that, I will give you some time. But make no mistake, Sonia, you are my wife and you had better start acting like it, and soon, or life will become very unpleasant for you."

A shiver travelled down Sonia's spine as she remembered the look in his eyes. The man was dead serious.

She had to find a way to get the hell out of here and take her son with her. If she could get to the airport and catch a flight back to the U.S., she could go off the grid. Technically, she'd be kidnapping her own child, but screw that. He was her son. He had grown inside her for nine months. The Hague Convention be damned. Joseph had no right to keep them prisoner in Liberia or to place them in danger by taking over the government.

She needed a good plan to make this happen. If he caught her, she'd lose her window of opportunity. Joseph would never trust her again to take her son out alone. And she didn't even want to think about what else might happen. She couldn't protect David if she were dead or severely injured. She swallowed.

Fatima walked into the family room. "Is everything all right, my lady? Is there anything you need?"

Yeah, I need information.

"Fatima, come and sit with me for a moment." Sonia patted the cushions of the couch next to her.

"Of course, my lady." Fatima took a seat.

"I told you to call me Sonia. I'll never get used to that title. So, what has my husband put on the agenda for me this week?"

"Well, there are a couple of public appearances he has scheduled for you to attend. One of them is the reception being held at the United States Embassy. Our relationship with the United States is very important to Liberia. They will be concerned about the coup and we will need to demonstrate that the government of Liberia is now stable," Fatima said.

"Stable? How can Liberia show stability when my husband overthrew the democratically elected president? How do you feel about this?" Sonia asked.

Fatima shrugged. "It is the way things are. I'm fortunate to be working with the president."

"I hear on the radio that there is still unrest in the countryside. I'm so scared Fatima. I read that at least one of Liberia's former presidents was killed in this place. Are we safe here? What's to stop someone else from trying to take over? What guaranties do we have that we'll get out alive if that happens?" Sonia asked.

"There are no guaranties, ma'am," Fatima said. "All we can do is pray."

Chapter XI

Fatima and Saye sat on the couch in the living room of the Saytumah family mansion having cocktails. Fatima was dressed in a red negligee.

"So, how are things at the Presidential mansion?" Saye asked.

"Not so good, I am afraid. The first lady grows more and more worried every day," she said.

"And well she should be. It was not enough for my brother to take over the family business and my father's position in the Liberian Ministry. No, he had to take over the entire country as well. The greedy bastard. It would serve him right if someone else executed a coup," Saye said.

"You are the first-born. You are the rightful heir. It should be you living in the Presidential mansion, not him," Fatima said

"Yes, and as soon as we put our plan into motion, that will happen," Saye said. "When my brother realizes that his son is not safe in Liberia, he will take his family back to America. My brother was kidnapped and tortured as a child. He will not want that for his son."

"And then you will take over and I will be at your side," Fatima said.

"Yes. You have been a very loyal ally," Saye said.

"Sonia is already very worried about their safety. I would not put it past her to attempt to flee the country. What if she does that before we can execute our plan?" Fatima asked.

"Joseph told me that he has forbidden her to take my nephew out of the country. We just have to make sure she doesn't. Enough shop talk. Come here. I require relaxation," Saye said. Fatima smiled, slid closer to him kissed him on the lips, then on his neck, and then down his chest before continuing her journey down his body.

***

Sonia paced back and forth in the family room of the Presidential mansion then threw herself onto the couch. She was completely frustrated. Her plan to get a message to her father had not worked out at all. Joseph had interrupted her conversation with General Peters and spirited her away just when she had worked up enough courage to say something to the man. It was almost as if Joseph knew what she was going to do.

The party at the Embassy had been a prime opportunity to get a message to her father through an Embassy official. Now, she'd have to wait until the next diplomatic event. Even then, there were no guarantees. Meanwhile, Joseph could try to force her

to fulfill her so-called wifely duties. She shuddered at
the thought.

She stood up and began pacing back and forth
again. No, she couldn't put herself through that. She
refused to join the ranks of those poor girls at the rape
crisis center. She had to get out of here. But how?

She needed to devise a plan to get herself and
David to the airport. Maybe she could check the
flights and buy the tickets online using a credit card
and then contact her father when she landed.

The week before, Joseph had let her take
David to the market in downtown Monrovia. The
driver had dropped them off at one end of the long
street and picked them up at the other end. David had
loved the market with all of its sights, sounds, smells
and throngs of people milling about. He'd been
talking about it nonstop ever since and demanding to
know when they would be going back.

Sonia stopped pacing as the plan began to
unfold in her mind. She could get the driver to take
them to the market. While there, she could buy outfits
for herself and David, change their clothes, hop into a
taxi – they were always available at the market – and
take it to the airport.

She flashed back to the look in Joseph's eyes
the night before and shook her head. It would never
work. He knew she'd intended to slip General Peters
a message. He knew she was plotting a way out of
this situation. If he knew she was planning to take
David out to the market without the nanny, he might
stop her or find some other way to thwart her plans.

She had to find a way to distract him. She walked back over to the couch and sat down.

Fatima entered the room. "My lady, can I get you anything?"

Sonia looked up at the woman and saw opportunity. Fatima had continued to be Joseph's administrative assistant even after he became the president of Liberia. Since part of her job duties entailed informing Sonia of events she was expected to attend as the first lady and coordinating her calendar, she'd become sort an assistant to Sonia as well.

Sonia didn't particularly like Fatima. She couldn't quite put her finger on it, but something about the woman's passive, obsequious manner turned her off. She just got a weird vibe from her. She was the last person Sonia wanted to rely upon for her escape plan to work. But she had no choice. Fatima was uniquely positioned to keep Joseph busy so that she and David could have the opportunity to escape.

Although they were never destined to become best friends, they had built up a sort of rapport in the weeks since the coup. And Fatima seemed particularly fond of David. Perhaps she could use that to enlist her help.

Sonia rose from the couch and walked over to Fatima. "I can't take it anymore."

Fatimah's brow furrowed. "What do you mean? What can't you take? Are you in pain, my lady? Is it one of your migraines? I will call the doctor." She turned toward the door and took a step.

Sonia reached out and grabbed her arm to stop her. She shook her head. "No. I don't have a migraine. I'm just going slowly mad. I can't keep smiling in everyone's face as if nothing were wrong when the truth is that I'm being kept hostage here in Liberia and my son is not safe. I have to do something about it."

"What do you mean? Who is holding you hostage?" Fatima asked.

"My husband will not let me take our son to safety in America. He says that if I leave him and go back to America to live, I'll never see my son again," Sonia said.

"Oh that is terrible, my lady!" Fatima dropped her head and started to wring her hands. "Such a young boy needs his mother. Surely you can find a way to stay here and be with him until he is old enough to go off to college? Who knows? By then, you and the President may get along better."

Sonia stared at Fatimah. *What? Stay here for another sixteen years? Is she out of her damned mind? If, by some fortune, we aren't killed before then, I'd wish I were dead. No. Who am I kidding? I'll have either slit my wrists or taken Joseph out in his sleep and gotten executed long before then.*

She realized that she was still staring at Fatima, her mouth wide open in astonishment. She snapped her jaw closed and shook her head. "No Fatimah. There's no way I can do that." She took Fatima by the arm and led her over to the couch.

"Look, I've figured out a way to get my son to America. But I need your help to do it."

"My help?" Fatima's eyes grew wide as saucers and she shook her head from side to side. "Oh I don't know, my lady. Mr. Saytumah would kill me if he even knew we were having this conversation. I could never go against his wishes. He is the president, not to mention my boss."

Sonia reached out and put her hand over Fatima's. "Fatima, do you have any children?"

"No yet, my lady. I pray one day to be blessed with them," Fatima said.

"Well, when you do have them, you'll discover that there's nothing you won't do to keep them safe. You know about the unrest here. If Joseph and I are killed in the next coup, what will happen to David? You have to help me, Fatima. I'm begging you." She squeezed Fatima's hand.

Fatima lowered her eyes and was silent for a moment, then she looked at Sonia and smiled. "He's such a beautiful little boy. I do want him to be safe. What can I do to help?"

Thank God.

"I've bought plane tickets to take me and David to America. He'll be safe there. I'll have the driver take us to the market in downtown Monrovia and then catch a taxi to the airport. I need for you to keep Joseph busy so he doesn't see us leave. If he sees me leaving with David, he may guess what I'm up to and stop me. Can you do that?"

"Yes ma'am. We have several very important meetings lined up this week. I can arrange to get Mr. Saytumah out of the house or, at the very least, keep him in his office on conference calls or in meetings while you get away. When are you planning to leave?" Fatima asked.

"Two days from now, at 2:00p.m. Oh Fatima! I'll find a way to repay you for your kindness. I know what kind of risk you're taking and I appreciate it. You're saving my son's life. I am forever grateful." She gave Fatima a hug. She'd underestimated the woman. Apparently, she had more heart and more backbone than Sonia had ever imagined.

"It is my pleasure. Your son is much too young to be kept in this sort of danger," Fatima said.

Sonia felt tears prick the back of her eyelids. "Thank you again, from the bottom of my heart.

Chapter XII

Two days later, Sonia entered the nursery and gave the nanny a sunny smile. "Hi there. How's my little man?"

The nanny returned the smile. "He is wonderful, ma'am. I just fed him lunch. He has a good appetite."

Sonia turned to watch David play with his new fire truck. He pushed it across the floor making loud engine noises. He loved that toy. She'd have to get him a new one once they got to the States. She turned back to the nanny. "I haven't been spending as much time with him lately, what with all the first lady responsibilities. I'd like to spend the rest of the day with him. There's no need for the two of us to be here. Why don't you take the rest of the day off and come back in the morning? I'll make sure you get paid for the whole day."

"Really ma'am? Are you sure you don't want me to stay or to come back in a few hours? It's no trouble at all."

"I am sure. Now go on. Live a little." Sonia smiled at the nanny to put her at ease.

"Thank you very much, ma'am." She did not have to be told twice; she gathered her things and left the nursery.

Sonia turned to her son. "Come here, sweetie." She crouched down to his height and opened her arms wide. David got up from the floor where he'd been playing and toddled over to her. She scooped him up and carried him to the door of the nursery. She opened it and looked up and down the hall. Seeing no-one, she carried her son to the master bedroom and set him down onto the bed while she grabbed her purse and a baby bag she had packed earlier.

David watched her, a big smile on his face. "We going out, Mommy?"

Dear Lord. If he got too excited and started announcing the fact that they were leaving to the world, they'd never get out. She should have drugged him or something. But no, she couldn't do that. What if she gave him too heavy a dose? She'd never forgive herself. She looked at him thoughtfully. There had to be some way of keeping him quiet for a few minutes. Maybe it was time they started playing the secrets game.

"Yes, baby," she said. "We're going out." She put her finger to her lips. "Shh! It's our secret. Don't tell anybody."

David put his little finger to his lips. "Shh."

She picked him up, gave him a kiss, left the master bedroom and quickly headed down the hall. When she got to the entrance of the living room, she stopped, put her back to the wall and peeked into the room. David kept his fingers to his lips and leaned forward trying to peek as well. The living room was empty as was the foyer.

She straightened and carried her son out the front door. Her driver was waiting outside. She'd told him earlier that she planned to take her son to the market.

"Are you ready to go, ma'am?" he asked.

"Yes, thank you," Sonia said.

David held a finger to her lips. "Shhh Mommy. It's a secret."

The driver smiled at him. "It's a secret young man?"

Oh great. This is what I get for playing a secrets game with a two year old.

She rolled her eyes and smiled at the driver. "Don't mind him. It's just a little game we were playing earlier."

She turned to David. "All right silly, no more secrets. Mr. Johnson knows we're going out. He's going to drive us to the market."

David's eyes lit up. "The market? Yay! I like the market, mommy," He clapped his little hands together.

Sonia sighed and glanced around to see if anyone was paying them any particular attention. No-one was. She strapped David into his car seat and they were off. She breathed a quiet sigh of relief as the car left the presidential compound.

David was still chattering about the market.

Sonia caught the driver's eye in the rearview mirror and smiled. "He just loves the market."

"Well then," the driver said, "let's get this little fellow to the market."

Traffic was at its usual crawl. The drive felt like it took forever. She kept thinking she would hear the driver's cell phone ring and someone would give him orders to turn around and take them back to the mansion.

When the car finally pulled up to the curb next to one of the market stands, she reached over and unhooked David from his car seat. "You don't have to wait around for us. Since he loves the place so much, I figure we'll shop for a while and then get something to eat. Plus, there are lots of kids here for him to play with. We'll meet you back here in a couple of hours."

The driver nodded. "Yes ma'am. I will pick you up right here in two hours. If you need me sooner, you can call me on my cell and I will get here right away."

Sonia smiled. "Sounds like a plan." She picked David up out of the car seat, set him down on the sidewalk, and closed the car door. "See you later."

"Yes ma'am." The car pulled away from the curb.

Wasting no time, Sonia took David by the hand and set off in search of a stall that sold children's clothing. She bought a new outfit for David and a little baseball cap. She stopped at a few more stalls and bought some things to change her appearance – a bright flowery sundress, large dark sunglasses that covered much of her face, a red wig. She took her purchases into the ladies' room where she and David did a quick change act. When she was done, she stuffed their old clothing into the baby bag and checked herself out in the mirror. She looked like a tourist from hell, but at least she looked nothing like herself. She smiled.

When she finished, she inspected her son. He looked adorable. He had fussed a little when she changed his clothes, but he loved his new hat. She told him they were playing dress-up.

"You look pretty, Mommy," he said.

"Thank you, sweetie." She picked him up and gave him a kiss.

They left the restroom and headed toward the street where the taxicabs were lined up. She motioned to one of the drivers. He pulled up and they climbed inside. He looked in the rearview mirror at Sonia and said something in a thick Liberian accent she didn't understand. She assumed he was asking her where she wanted to go.

"I need to go to the airport," she said. "I'll pay the full fare. We're in a hurry and don't have time for you to pick up more passengers."

"You are American yes?" the driver asked.

Sonia nodded. "Yes. We are American."

"I know. You Americans are always in a hurry – especially in New York," he said. "Do you know New York?"

"Yes, I know New York." Sonia smiled. Taxicab drivers were the same all over the world. She could have been in New York. The driver would fit right in with all the other taxicab drivers there with thick accents. She sat back and relaxed for a second. She and David were on their way to the airport. So far, her plan was working.

She'd have to go into hiding. Despite what he had done, Joseph still had parental rights. The last thing she needed was for him to win custody of David or have her arrested for kidnapping her own son. She knew the kidnapping would not look good to a family court judge.

She also ran the risk of Joseph taking a more direct route. She didn't doubt for a second that he was capable of having her and David snatched and forcibly returned to Liberia. There was a large Liberian community in New York. Any one of them might be looking to curry a little favor with the president of Liberia.

She looked down at her son who had fallen asleep in her arms and kissed him on the forehead. She couldn't take that chance. She'd have to find a way to disappear and find a new life. She had some savings and she knew her parents would help. She didn't quite know how she'd go about it, but she'd find a way. She just had to stay off the grid. She and David would never be safe as long as Joseph was alive. He would never stop searching for his son or the wife who had betrayed him.

The taxicab pulled up to the airport terminal. She paid the driver and got out, then walked into the airport carrying her son.

***

Joseph sat at his desk in the Presidential office, studying reports on his computer screen. The military appeared to be making good progress in quelling the few dissidents who refused to accept his rule.

The telephone rang. After a moment, Fatima buzzed him.

"Sir, it is the Liberian press. They want to know if you are sending your wife and son out of the country as a result of the growing unrest in the countryside," she said.

"What? What are they talking about?" Joseph asked.

"Well sir, according the reporter, the first lady has purchased plane tickets to New York for herself and David. Their flight leaves this evening at six o'clock," she said.

He leapt to his feet. "What? Where is she now?"

"I saw her get into her car about an hour ago," Fatima said.

"Did she have my son with her?" Joseph asked.

"Yes," Fatima said.

Joseph's heart sank. He glanced at his watch. It was 4:00p.m. It would take him almost an hour to get to the airport.

"Sir, what shall I tell the reporter?"

"Tell them that my wife and son are not leaving the country and that I have no further comment. Then put me through to airport security. Also, tell my driver to get the car ready. We are going to the airport," Joseph said.

***

David was fussy as a result of having his nap interrupted. Sonia consoled him as best she could. She handed their tickets to the flight attendant. She had bought first class tickets so that they could be among the first to board the plane and she could make David as comfortable as possible during the long flight. The flight attendant looked at the tickets, hesitated for a moment, and then plastered a smile onto her face.

Sonia felt her heart leap into her throat. She knew there was a chance her husband would find out about the flight and try to stop her. "Is there a problem?"

"No ma'am," the woman said. "If you would please wait here for just a moment." She stepped over to the desk, picked up the telephone and spoke in a native Liberian dialect.

Moments later, a Liberian solder appeared. He looked at Sonia and David. "I am afraid you will have to come with me, ma'am."

Dear God no.

Sonia felt herself starting to panic. Anger took over and she decided to try and bluff her way out. "What do you mean? What's this about? We've already gone through security. I'm not going anywhere with you. We'll miss our flight. Do you know who I am?"

The soldier nodded, a hint of a smile playing around his lips. "Yes ma'am. I have orders to escort you to security. Please come with me or I will be forced to detain you."

"Detain me? Have you lost your mind? You will regret this. When my husband gets through with you, there will be nothing left."

The soldier remained impassive. "Right this way, ma'am." He put one hand on his weapon and swept the other in front of him.

David began to whimper. Sonia picked him up, glared at the soldier, and then followed him to a door. He opened it, but did not follow her in. Joseph waited inside a small office.

He turned to the soldier and nodded. "Thank you," he said. "You are dismissed."

The soldier saluted and left.

Joseph turned to her. The look in his eye caused Sonia's mouth to dry out. He looked murderous.

She swallowed. "Joseph, what are you doing here?"

"I could ask the same thing of you except I know what you are doing here. How dare you? How dare you try to steal my son from me and smuggle him out of the country? I told you that David is a Liberian and his place is here with me."

Anger burned away the fear and gave her the courage to lash back at him. "How dare I? How dare you keep us here with all the unrest in this country? How dare you place me and David in danger of getting shot any minute when the next coup happens? What did you expect me to do? I had to do something to keep him safe. I'm his mother, and his father's not thinking of his best interests."

Joseph stared at her through narrowed eyes. "I see that you cannot be trusted." His voice was eerily quiet. "I am placing you and David under guard. If you ever try to take my son from me again, I will kill you. Do you understand me? You and he belong to me. There is no leaving. You had better resign yourself to that fact and make the best of it or I will make your life a living hell. You American woman are too spoiled. You need a firm hand to rein you in. Don't worry. I've got exactly what you need."

"What the hell does that mean?" she asked. "What are you going to do? Lock me up in a dungeon and feed me bread and water? Oh yeah, that'll go over well in the international community. I can see the headlines now."

"You'll see. I've given you way too much leeway. That ends today. Now, we are going back home. If you make a scene, I will simply knock you out and carry you. Which way do you want to go? Walking or not?"

Sonia stared at him, looking for some semblance of the man she had fallen in love with. There was no sign of him in Joseph's furious gaze. "I'll cooperate. There's no need for violence."

Joseph nodded. "You've made a wise choice. Let's go."

***

As soon as they got back to the mansion, Joseph called the nanny and ordered her to take David. He then grabbed Sonia by the arm and marched her into the master bedroom. When she resisted, he backhanded her. Pain exploded across her face. The blow drove her backward.

She fell onto the bed. Joseph climbed on top of her and began ripping off her clothes. When she struggled, he backhanded her again. Stunned by the blow, she didn't move as he stripped her naked. He flipped her over and clicked her wrists and ankles into restraints that had already been attached to the bedposts. After he restrained her, he left the room.

Her mind raced as she lay there, face down on the bed, naked and spread—eagled. She had no idea what Joseph had in mind for her, but it couldn't be good. He'd never treated her so roughly before.

She wondered where the restraints had come from. Since they were already attached to the bed, it was clear Joseph had been planning to use them.

How had he found out about her escape plan? She started to run through possible scenarios, but her mind froze when Joseph stalked into the bedroom carrying a thick leather strap. He stood by the side of the bed and looked down at her, running the leather through his hands. Sonia shivered.

"It's time to teach you a lesson in obedience," he said. "I cannot have my wife disobeying my orders if I expect obedience from my troops and the citizens of Liberia."

"Joseph, please don't." Sonia struggled against the bonds.

"You should have thought about the consequences when you dreamed up the scheme to flee the country with my son. I think fifty licks should do the trick." He raised the belt high and swung down hard with it. It cracked against Sonia's buttocks, leaving a trail of fire in its wake. She screamed and kept on screaming as it came down again and again, over her back, her buttocks, and the backs of her legs.

.

Chapter XIII

The nanny sat on a bench knitting and keeping a watchful eye on David who played with his brand new puppy on the grass. She looked up at the clear blue sky. It was a beautiful day. The brightness of the sun, the boy's peals of laughter and the puppy's happy barks contrasted sharply with the guards patrolling the presidential compound with machine guns.

The guards became less visible for a very brief period at four o'clock in the afternoon when the shift change took place and there was a one minute gap in their rotation at that portion of the compound. Taking advantage of the gap, a man, who seemed to materialize out of thin air, appeared and snatched David off the grass. He clapped a hand over the boy's mouth and ran off. David kicked and struggled to no avail. The kidnapper carried him out of the compound and jumped into a waiting Jeep which sped off with squealing tires.

The nanny sat there, frozen, for at least ten seconds before sounding the alarm. She screamed. "Help! Help! They took him! They took him!"

Guards come running up to her from all directions. One of them took her by the shoulders and shook her. "What are you talking about? Who took who?"

"A man came in here and took the presidents' son! It happened so fast I could not believe it! He left in a jeep," she said.

The guard turned to give orders to the others. "Bring the cars around and go after that jeep." He turned back to the nanny. "Which way did it go?"

"It went west. Oh my God. The president will kill me! It's all my fault. It's all my fault! That poor little boy." She put her head into her hands and sobbed.

The guard shook her again. "Pull yourself together! We have to go tell the President what happened." He took her by the arm and all but dragged her to the Presidential office. Once there, he approached one of the President's personal guards outside the door. "We need to see the President. It is urgent. His son has been kidnapped."

The President's man nodded and knocked on the door to the office. Fatima opened it. After a brief exchange, she ushered them inside.

***

Joseph, who had been talking on the telephone with a Chinese dignitary, looked up. The sight of the sobbing nanny caused his heart to leap up into his throat. He did not see David with her. "I have to go," he said into the telephone. "An emergency has arisen. Yes, I will make the arrangements and call you tomorrow. Goodbye."

He hung up and looked up at the sobbing nanny. If she didn't give him some satisfactory answers, quickly, he would give her something to cry about. "Where is my son? Why is he not with you?"

The nanny stopped sobbing and cowered. "They . . . they took him."

Joseph rose from his seat, came around the large desk, grabbed the woman by her arms, and shook her. "What do you mean they took him? Who took him?"

"I don't know, sir. A man ran onto the grounds and took him. I have never seen him before." The nanny started to sob all over again.

Joseph glared at her. She had to give them more information than this or they would never find his son. That was not an option. "It was your job to protect him. What were you doing while my son was being kidnapped?"

"I was watching him. I swear. I was sitting on a bench not more than five feet away. One minute he was happy, playing with his new puppy, and the next minute he was gone. I froze. I could not believe what was happening," she said.

Joseph turned to the guard. "Take her into custody. I want her interrogated thoroughly. Then I want you to take a contingent of men and find my son. Do not come back here without him. Do you understand me?"

"Yes sir," the guard said. He took the now hysterical nanny by the arm and yanked her out of the Presidential office.

Joseph turned to Fatima. "Bring my wife here please."

Fatima nodded and left the office.

Joseph sat on the edge of his desk, put his head into his hands and wondered what he could possibly say to his wife. She was right. He had put their family in mortal danger with his blind ambition. And now his son -- a sweet, innocent two year old boy -- was about to pay the price.

He must be terrified. The thought made Joseph sick and filled him with an impotent rage. He walked over to a filing cabinet and kicked it viciously, creating a huge dent in the metal. If he ever got his hands on the kidnappers he would tear them limb from limb. How dare they take his son from him? How dare they make David feel the terror he had felt when he had been kidnapped all those years ago? At least he had been twelve. David was still a baby.

***

Sonia rushed into the Presidential office. Fatima said that something had happened to David and that Joseph wanted to see her. She wouldn't say what happened. Joseph stood next to his desk, seemingly lost in thought.

"What's wrong?" She could barely get the words out over her pounding heart. She could barely breathe.

Joseph looked up at her, but did not speak.

She walked over to him. "Where's David?" She looked around the office hoping David would jump out from behind one of the desks and surprise her. It was one of his favorite games lately.

"There has been a problem," Joseph said. "Please sit down." He took her by the arm and led her to one of the chairs in front of his desk.

She sat down. "Problem? What kind of problem?'

"It's David. He has been kidnapped," Joseph said.

Sonia leapt up out of her chair. "What? What do you mean kidnapped? I just saw him an hour ago. He was in the nursery. What happened?"

Joseph took her by the shoulders. "Sonia, please calm down."

Sonia shrugged his hands off. "Don't you tell me to calm down, you bastard! I told you this would happen! I tried to protect him – take him away from this madness -- and you stopped me. This is all your fault! I hate you! I hate you!" She curled her hand into fists and pummeled him with them until he grabbed her by the wrists, pulled her close to him and held her.

She sobbed against his chest for a moment, then pulled away. "My son. My poor baby. He's so little. Oh God, oh God, oh God, please let him be safe. You've got to find him. They could kill him, just to get back at you."

The very thought sent so much pain coursing through her that she collapsed into a chair in a frenzy of sobs.

Joseph turned to the guard standing next to him. "Go get the doctor. I want him to give my wife a sedative."

Sonia looked up at her husband. She didn't know she could feel such hatred for anyone. She wanted to grab the letter opener lying on his desk and stab him through the neck with it. But that would have to wait. He had a job to do and that was to bring their son back alive. He may be a complete bastard, but he did love his son. She knew he would move heaven and Earth to get him back.

"I don't want a sedative. I want my son back. I don't give a fuck who you have to torture, maim or kill. You find my son and bring him back to me. Do you hear me, you bastard? Bring me back my son."

"I will bring him back. I promise you that." He reached out to touch her face, but she slapped his hand away and stalked out of the office.

***

Later that afternoon, General Maconda and his men advanced slowly toward a small house on the outskirts of Monrovia. It was little more than a shack just off a dirt road. They had watched the house for a while before commencing their approach. There did not appear to be any outside sentries.

When they got to the house, the soldiers flattened themselves against it. The general peered through a window and saw four men inside. He looked back at his men and held up four fingers. He signaled for two of them to go around to the back of the house and for two others to follow him through the front door. On his signal, one of his men kicked the door in.

He entered, going low, his men following behind him. The hostiles turned in surprise as the door crashed open. Before they could raise their weapons, he had fired and taken out one of them. His men made short work of the rest.

He heard a child crying. The sound came from the back room. He rushed inside to find one of his men holding the president's son in his arms. Another one of his men entered the back door of the shack dragging one of the kidnappers by the arm.

"I found this one trying to escape out the back," he said.

The general looked at the prisoner who cowered under his gaze. He leaned in until his face was very close to the prisoner's and looked him in the eye.

"There is no escape for you. By the time I get done with you, you will have told me everything I need to know. And you will beg for the escape of death," he said.

The prisoner's eyes grew wide and he began to struggle with the soldier holding him. The soldier pistol whipped him. Stunned, the prisoner sagged in his grasp. The soldier dragged him outside.

The general took the president's son from the soldier and cradled the child against him until he stopped crying and stared up at him with wide tear-soaked eyes.

"Are you okay?" the general asked.

David nodded his little head

The general smiled at him. "Good boy." He strode out of the house with the child.

*****

Joseph put down the telephone handset, closed his eyes, and sagged against the back of his chair, relief flooding through him. His son was alive. It was more than he could ask. He would tell Sonia when she awoke. The last time he checked, she had still been knocked out from the sedative he had the doctor give her. She had been dead set against taking the shot and had fought them tooth and nail. Literally. He rubbed at the bite marks on his arm and smiled. That woman was a hellcat. She needed to be tamed and he was just the man to do it.

The door to the Presidential office opened and the general strode in holding David.

"Daddy!" David smiled happily and held out his little arms for his father to take him.

"Son." Joseph jumped up out of his seat and jogged across the room. He took his son from the general and held him close. The little boy burrowed his face into his neck. After a moment, Joseph pulled back and inspected him. He did not appear to have any visible bruises or injuries. "I am so happy to see you. Are you okay? Did they harm you?" His voice shook a little.

David shook his head. "No Daddy. I was scared." His little face crumpled and tears streamed down his cheeks.

Joseph hugged him again. "I know baby. I know." He looked up at the general. "Where was he?"

"They were holding him in a small house right outside Monrovia. There were four kidnappers. Three of them are dead. We brought one back for interrogation," the general said.

"How did you find him?"

"Before she died, the nanny confessed that it was her brother who had taken the child. She knew where they were holding him. She had planned to sneak out later to check on him."

"Did she say who was behind this?" Joseph asked.

"She said that Fatima set up the kidnapping," the general said.

"Fatima?" Joseph could scarcely believe his ears. He'd known Fatima all of her life. They'd grown up together. Their families were close. The shock soon turned to rage. "Fatima did this? Where is she now?"

"We searched the mansion and the grounds. She does not appear to be here," the general said. "We also searched her home, but, so far, we have not been able to locate her."

"Find that bitch and bring her to me," Joseph said through clenched teeth.

Yes sir." The general saluted and left.

***

Sonia woke up with her mouth feeling as dry as the Sahara Desert. Her tongue felt as if it had a layer of fur on it. She licked her cracked lips and pushed herself up into a sitting position. That's when she discovered the horrible headache. She put the back of her hand against her head, slumped back against the headboard, and looked around.

How long had she been out? She glanced at the window and squinted at the red and orange rays that signaled the imminent setting of the African sun.

What the hell had happened? The last thing she remembered was fighting with her husband and the needle going into her arm. Then it all came flooding back. Her heart sped up.

David.

She had just thrown her leg over the side of the bed when the bedroom door opened and David came running into the room. "Mommy, mommy, you're awake!"

Sonia couldn't believe her eyes. Was she dreaming? Was she having a drug-induced hallucination? Had the stress of all this finally caused her to lose her mind? She watched, motionless as her son leapt up onto the bed and launched himself at her. She caught him and clutched him to her chest, burrowing her face into his hair. His little arms clutched at her neck.

"Oh baby, you're safe." She pulled him back and planted kisses all over his face. David squirmed and giggled. It was the most beautiful sound she'd ever heard. She pulled him close again and looked up at the ceiling. "Thank you God. Thank you, thank you, thank you." Tears of joy streamed down her face.

"Don't cry, mommy." David's voice quivered.

She hadn't meant to upset him. She wiped her face and smiled at him to put him at ease. "Mommy's crying because she's so happy to see you."

She caught movement out of the corner of her eye and looked up. Joseph stood there, leaning against the doorjamb, watching them. She stared back at him coldly until finally, he nodded and left. She checked David all over for injuries; thankfully, he didn't seem to have any – not physical ones anyway. She held him close and listened to him chatter about puppies and toys and bad men.

Never again.

They'd been lucky this time. But neither she nor David could afford to risk this ever happening again. She'd do whatever it took to get her son out of danger -- even if that meant killing his father.

Chapter XIV

A few weeks later, Sonia, Tara and Tyrone sat in the living room of the Nkrumah family mansion. Tara rambled on about the last guy she'd dated. Tyrone cracked jokes about how she had probably scared him off by acting like a mother hen.

Sonia looked out the window to check on the guard Joseph had assigned to her. He was outside, chatting with her driver. Good. He wouldn't be able hear what she was about to say. She turned back to Tara and Tyrone. "Listen, I have to talk to you about something."

Tara stopped talking midsentence and stared at her.

"I'm sorry," Sonia said. "I don't mean to be rude. And I'm taking a huge risk with you being such close friends with the Saytumah family, but I don't know where else to turn."

Tara reached out and patted Sonia on the shoulder. "You know you can talk to us about anything, Sonia. Please tell us what's wrong."

"Well, ever since Joseph executed the coup, I've been so scared. With all the unrest here, I keep thinking that, at any moment, someone else will try to take over the country and kill us all," Sonia said.

"Have you talked to Joseph about this?" Tara asked.

"Yes, of course I have. On the day the coup happened, I confronted him. He never discussed it with me – he just did it with no regard whatsoever for the danger it would bring to our family. On that day, I found out that this had been his plan all along," she said.

"Oh my goodness! You poor dear. That must have been terrible. How could he have done that?" Tara asked.

"You don't know the half of it. I told him I wanted to leave. He said that I could leave, but I couldn't take David with me. I couldn't believe it. How could I leave David here? So I tried to escape and take David with me. Joseph caught up with us at the airport," Sonia said.

Tara winced. "Ooh. That can't have been good,"

Sonia grimaced. "No. It wasn't good at all. He – he tied me down and whipped me and started treating me like a prisoner. He puts guards on me and monitors my every move. I can't go anywhere without them. Despite all the extra security, David got kidnapped right off the front lawn. I thought I would die." She paused for a moment to try and keep it together. "I was so terrified of what they'd do to him. Luckily, Joseph's men found him quickly and he seems to be all right. He doesn't have any physical injuries. Thank God. But what emotional scars will he carry as a result of this?' Her breath caught on a sob.

Tara took her hand and squeezed it. Sonia looked down at her lap and was silent for a moment until she got herself under control again, then she looked up at them. "I can't live like this. I've got to get us back to the States, where David will be safe. Doing that is next to impossible now that we're under guard all the time. What am I going to do?"

Tara and Tyrone looked at each other. Tara nodded. Tyrone turned to face Sonia.

"Sonia, there's something we need to tell you. Tara and I are not who you think we are."

Sonia stared at him. *What? Tell me he did not just say what I think he just said. Is anyone in this godforsaken place who they're supposed to be? Where am I – in the goddamn Twilight Zone? Easy girl. Maybe you should just hear him out. And maybe it's best if you don't. Maybe you should just get the hell out of here while the getting is good before they make any revelations they can't take back.* But leaving meant going back to the Presidential mansion – back to the danger zone. If she ever wanted to get away from that place, she needed their help.

"What do you mean?" she asked.

"Tara and I are agents for the U.S. government. We've been undercover here in Liberia for the past few years," he said.

"Undercover? I don't understand. Why?"

"We've been watching the Saytumah family. They run one of the largest and most organized arms dealing operations in the world," Tyrone said.

Sonia sat up, leaned forward and slapped her hands onto her thighs. "What?" It came out more like a screech.

She felt Tara grab hold of one of her wrists. When she turned to look at her, Tara put a finger to her lips and inclined her head toward the window. Sonia looked. The guard was outside having a cigarette. She looked at Tara and nodded to signal that she understood then turned back to Tyrone.

"Yes, I'm afraid it's true," he said. "Before he died, Dwe was positioning himself to execute a coup and take over the country. We knew that. What we didn't know was that Joseph would take up where his daddy left off."

Sonia could scarcely believe what she was hearing. But it all made a sick kind of sense. Hadn't she always suspected that Joseph's business trips for his father's company were for nefarious purposes? Hadn't she suspected him of being up to no good when he showed up, out of the blue, at her law firm after ten years? Well, it turned out her instincts were correct.

She'd never dreamed how bad Joseph really was. She'd let hormones and kinky sex get in the way of her judgment and now, she and her son were paying the price. She'd been an easy mark for the sexy, exotic and powerful man that was her husband. She'd been exactly what he needed when he needed it

– willing sex partner, top notch negotiator, loving wife, mother to his heir and a senator's daughter with great political connections in America. The full depth of his deception became clear to her at that moment. She felt so stupid, so used.

She rose from her seat on the couch, crossed her arms and began pacing the living room floor. "That fucking bastard." She hissed the words through clenched teeth to keep from screaming them. "He played me. He played me like a damned violin from the very beginning and I was stupid enough to fall for it even when though I knew – I knew something wasn't right. When we were in college, I suspected Joseph and his father's company of being involved in something illegal like selling drugs. I had no idea they were arms dealers. He was always so mysterious about his father's business. But, when he came to my firm for legal work, I had him and the company checked out thoroughly. We turned up nothing."

"That's because the Saytumah family is very good at covering their tracks. They're been under investigation by several U.S. government agencies, Interpol and the Mossad for years. None of us have ever gathered enough evidence to take them down. That's where we need your help," Tyrone said.

Sonia stopped pacing and stared at him. "My help? What do you mean?"

"He means that we could help each other," Tara said. "Tyrone and I can arrange for you and your son to travel back to the U.S. on a Red Cross flight. In exchange, you'll help us get the evidence we need to take the Saytumah family down."

"What exactly would I have to do?" Sonia asked.

"We need to get copies of the Saytumah family's computer files -- details of their transactions, operations and holdings. We'll provide you with a gadget to connect to your husband's computer system so we can download the information. Joseph has a standalone system that can't be hacked from the outside. But, if someone on the inside could help us, then we could get what we need," Tyrone said.

"You've been to the Saytumah family mansion many times and the Presidential mansion. Joseph trusts you. Why haven't you been able to get into his computer system?" Sonia asked.

Tara looked at her brother and smiled. "I told you she was smart." She turned to Sonia. "We couldn't afford to break our cover in the event we got caught, so we sneaked another operative inside the Saytumah family mansion during Dwe's birthday celebration. Unfortunately, Saye almost caught him. He couldn't allow himself to be captured since that would have jeopardized the operation so he jumped off a balcony from one of the rooms on the west side of the mansion." Tara paused and looked down. A single tear slid down her cheek. She wiped it away. "They found his body down the beach where it washed ashore. He was my protégé."

Tyrone rose from his seat and joined his sister on the couch. He put an arm around her shoulders and looked up at Sonia. "So you see," he said, "we really need your help. We need to make sure Jared didn't die in vain."

Sonia started pacing again and tried to think. It was hasty decisions that had brought her to this point. Her next move would have to be carefully thought out. Both her life and David's depended upon it. Right now, helping the CIA seemed like her only option. But that didn't matter if it would get her killed. If she did this, Joseph would kill her. She and David would have to disappear permanently. "Joseph has already caught me once trying to smuggle David out of the country. He said he'd kill me if I tried that again. He'll definitely kill me if he finds out I've done this. How can you guaranty our safety?" she asked.

"After we get the evidence, we can arrest Joseph and bring him back to the U.S. where he will be tried on criminal charges and for war crimes. He'll never be free again. We'll also arrange for you and your son to go into the witness protection program," Tyrone said.

That promise was only good if she was able to complete the mission undetected. If she failed at that, she was as good as dead. She'd be unable to protect her son. But what choice did she really have? She shook her head and started pacing again. "I don't know. I'd do anything to get David out of Liberia and to safety, but this seems so risky. What if Joseph or one of his guards catches me in the act?"

"We'll supply you with a communication device and be listening the entire time from a nearby location," Tara said. "As soon as we receive the information, we'll come to the mansion to take Joseph into custody. You will have to use your wiles to survive until then."

Sonia stopped pacing and turned to stare at Tara. *Use my wiles? Is this bitch crazy?* Her thoughts must have been all over her face because she could have sworn she saw Tara's lips twitch slightly.

"We'll provide you with a weapon to use in case of extreme emergency," Tyrone said. "Have you ever fired a gun before?"

"I've been to a shooting range once or twice with friends and fired guns, but I never dreamed of actually having to use one in self-defense," Sonia said.

"We have a shooting range downstairs. You can practice there until you feel comfortable," Tara said. "We'll also show you some basic self-defense moves you can use if you get into a jam."

"You have a shooting range downstairs? Won't the driver and the guard hear the gunshots if we start shooting down there?" Sonia asked.

"No. The room is soundproofed," Tara said. "Come with me. I'll show you."

Sonia followed Tara out of the living room and into the study. Tara went behind the large mahogany desk, slid her fingers underneath and pressed a hidden button. The bookshelves on the wall to the left of the desk slid aside to reveal a set of stairs.

Sonia's jaw dropped. She'd only seen such things in spy movies. She followed Tara and Tyrone down the stairs which led to a hallway. Tara pulled a set of keys from the pocket of her skirt and inserted one into the lock in a door on the right-hand side. She opened the door, reached in, and flipped on a light switch. Inside was a firing range, complete with targets.

Sonia looked around in astonishment. She followed Tara to a door on the far side of the room. Tara used another key on her ring to open it. It was closet holding a veritable armory. Guns ranging from small pistols to machine guns hung in slots along the back wall of the closet. Boxes of what Sonia assumed was ammunition were lined up neatly on a shelf. What appeared to be hand grenades were stacked in a neat little row. Below that was what looked like a grenade launcher. Sonia couldn't be sure since she'd only seen these types of weapons in movies. The reality was far different.

Tara reviewed her choices, glanced back at Sonia and removed a handheld gun from its slot. It wasn't the smallest of the handguns, but it wasn't the largest one, either. She grabbed a box of bullets and turned back to Sonia.

Sonia looked at the gun and swallowed in an attempt to lubricate her suddenly dry mouth. "Is that for me?"

"Yes. This should do the trick," Tara said. "Let's load this puppy and see what you can do with it." She led Sonia over to one of the stations. "Now, this is how you load the gun. She selected a clip from the box and slammed it home. She then pulled back the hammer, sliding one bullet into the chamber.

As Sonia watched her, the reality of what she was being asked to do hit her. She felt her heartbeat pick up speed. Panic nearly closed her throat. She had to clear it twice before getting words out. "Oh my God. I've never shot a human being before. What if I freeze? What if I can't do this? I'll be caught and killed and David will grow up in Liberia without a mother – assuming he gets to grow up at all."

Tara put the gun down onto the counter, gripped Sonia by the shoulders and gave her a little shake. "What will happen if you don't?   You and David will remain here, under constant danger, until you are eventually killed. Is that what you want?"

Sonia shook her head. *No. Hell no. Not if I can help it.*

She needed to be strong – to make the right choices this time. She didn't know if becoming a CIA asset and taking on a task this dangerous was the right choice. She'd read too many spy novels and seen too many action movies to think she was anything but expendable to them. They'd help her as long as she was useful, but they wouldn't blow their cover or compromise the mission to get her and David out. It wasn't the best situation, but she needed all the help she could get. If they wanted to give her a weapon and show her how to use it, then let them. She might need it one day. She'd decide what to do later after she could think it through.

She straightened her shoulders and nodded. "Okay, show me how to use it."

Tara nodded her approval. She picked up the gun and ejected the clip. "Okay. It's your turn to load it."

Tara made Sonia load and unload the gun several times until she got the hang of it. She also showed Sonia how to lock and unlock the safety on the gun. Next, she had Sonia practice firing the gun at the targets. The first few rounds Sonia fired missed the targets altogether, but with Tara's patient instruction and more practice, Sonia finally fired a few rounds into the target.

***

Over the next few weeks, Sonia visited the Nkrumah family mansion and worked with Tara and Tyrone on target practice and basic self-defense. She thought for sure her husband would notice how sore she was from working out with them, but he seemed distant and distracted whenever he was around her, and, to her relief, not very interested in sex.

"Today, I'm going to teach you about pressure points," Tyrone said.

"I've heard about that," Sonia said. "They're supposedly sensitive points on a person's body that when hit, will disable an attacker, right?"

Tyrone eyed her with approval. "That's right. Where did you learn that from?"

Sonia waved a hand at him. "You know, from watching action movies and such. Also, after September 11, I went a little insane and bought a battery-operated stun gun and some self-defense videos. I don't know what I thought I was doing. I guess I needed to take some measure of self-control to make sense of what happened. I figured if we were going to be attacked by foreigners, I needed to know how to defend myself. That didn't last long. I watched the videos but I didn't practice or take any self-defense courses. I kept the stun gun though," she said. "I kept it in the nightstand drawer next to my bed."

"Good girl." Tyrone grinned at her.

Sonia wondered why the idea of her keeping a stun gun in her nightstand drawer would cause him to grin at her like that. He was probably having kinky thoughts about stun guns and sex games. She needed to put an end to that. The last thing she needed was for him to be distracted during her training. She stared back at him with a serious expression on her face.

He cleared his throat and got back to the matter at hand. "Anyway, there are certain pressure points on a person's body you can access during an attack. For example, if someone grabs you from behind, you can stomp on the instep of their foot to distract them and then slam your elbow into their ribs right here." He pointed to a location on his body.

Sonia raised her eyebrows. "This could come in handy one day."

"Yes it could," he said. "There are also some pressure points in the head and neck areas. For example, if you take the heel of your hand and hit someone as hard as you can on an upward angle under their nose, you can do a lot of damage. You'll certainly cause pain and watery eyes. If you hit hard enough, you can break their nose or even kill them by pushing the bone and cartilage up into their brain. In any event, a good hit there should stop your attacker long enough for you to get away. If you can't get away, it will give you an opportunity to do further damage. You could, for example, follow up with a blow to the top of their head here with a heavy object or kick them in the groin."

Sonia shook her head. The thought of actually killing someone made her feel queasy. This was real - - not some action movie. *What the hell have I gotten myself into?*

"I guess you guys have to learn this stuff in your line of work. It just seems so violent," she said.

"Sonia, if you get cornered by an attacker and have to fight your way out, this stuff could very well save your life," he said.

"I know," she said. "I guess the truth of what I've gotten myself into is finally coming home to me. It's one thing to watch spy movies and fantasize about being the heroine. It's another thing altogether to know that I could be in harm's way any moment now and that it's my choices that put me and David there in the first place."

Tyrone gave her a sympathetic look. "This is not your fault. It Joseph's fault for putting you in the midst of this mess."

"But it is my fault," she said. "I knew better than to get involved with Joseph. I never trusted him completely. I should have trusted my instincts." She shrugged. "Looking back, I guess I was attracted to his bad boy persona. He always seemed exotic and sexy and powerful to me. I had no idea that he would turn into a megalomaniacal dictator of a third world country."

"The Saytumah family has been into gunrunning for generations," he said. "Although we had our suspicions, we've never been able to gather enough evidence put them out of business. Every agent that has tried to infiltrate their organization has been caught and killed. The shipping company acquisition gave them a new way to transport their weapons. It also helped them to expand their business operations. We believe that they're now transporting shipments for other gunrunners. That's the information we're hoping you'll be able to retrieve from his computer. If we know when the next shipment will take place, we can intercept it and have the proof we need to shut them down."

Sonia rolled her eyes. Just great. The fact that every other fool they'd sent in to get this information had been captured and/or killed made her feel much better about the assignment. Maybe she should rethink this. She couldn't protect David or get him out of the country if she got caught and killed. She didn't doubt for a moment Joseph would kill her if he ever found out she'd been the one to give this information to the CIA.

But she'd thought it over thoroughly over the past few weeks and had come to the conclusion that she didn't really have any other option. Helping the CIA and going into witness protection was really the best way to protect David. What she needed to do was to make sure David would be safe no matter what happened. She turned to Tyrone.

"Listen," she said, "I'll do this. I'm willing to take this risk. But the CIA has to promise me something -- and I want it in writing. You have to promise me that no matter what happens, if I try and get you this information and get captured and/or killed, the CIA will take David out of Liberia, give him to my parents, and put them all into witness protection."

Tyrone nodded. "You're a very brave woman, Sonia. I can't make any promises, but I'll see what I can do."

"You do that," Sonia said, "because those are the terms of my agreement to help the CIA. If I don't get that, we're all just wasting our time."

She knew she was asking for a lot. She was basically asking the CIA to kidnap the son of a foreign dignitary and to hide him from his father for the rest of his life. It was illegal and possibly immoral. But it was for his own good. The CIA would balk, but they would eventually give in. By Tyrone's account, they'd been trying to bring the Saytumahs down for more than twenty years. They needed her as much as she needed them.

Chapter XV

Two weeks later, Tara and Sonia got in some target practice.

"That's good," Tara said. "Just relax your shoulders and visualize the bullet going into the target. You want to squeeze the trigger. Don't jerk the gun, just aim it, hold it steady and squeeze the trigger."

Sonia barely stopped herself from rolling her eyes. Tara had been saying the same exact words for weeks. At least now Sonia was starting to get a feel for what the words actually meant. She focused her mind on the target, visualized the bullet hitting it, aimed the gun and squeezed the trigger while holding the gun as still as possible. The bullet hit the center mass of the target. For the first time in weeks, Sonia began to feel a measure of confidence in her shooting.

"That's it. Yes! Good girl." Tara clapped her hands together, drew them under her chin and beamed at Sonia. "Your shooting is getting so much better. You're now consistently hitting the target."

Sonia shot for a while longer until Tara signaled for her to stop. "Okay. Today, we're going to let you take the gun with you. Here are two extra clips. We're also going to give you some equipment you're going to need to download the information from your husband's computer."

Tara handed Sonia two gun clips and a tiny plastic-covered gadget. "This is a disc drive. It's loaded with a special program designed to both upload and download the contents of your husband's hard drive. Just plug it into a USB port on the computer. The drive will do the rest."

"How long will it take to finish downloading the data?" Sonia asked.

"That depends on how much data is on the computer. No longer than twenty minutes though," Tara said.

"Twenty minutes? That's a long time to be hanging out in the presidential office waiting to get caught," Sonia said.

Tyrone walked into the room. Apparently, he'd heard Sonia's remark because he responded. "We're going to be right there with you all the way." He held up something that looked like a tiny hearing aid. "This here is a communication device. When you hit the little button here and put this in your ear, we'll be able to hear everything you hear. We'll also be able to talk to you."

Oh great. So they'd be able to listen to her get caught and killed.

Stop that. Focus, she reminded herself. This is the job she'd signed up to do. And she'd do it well. She had to -- for David's sake.

After some back and forth, she'd finally wrangled a written agreement from the CIA. Her father helped secure that, no doubt. Tyrone and Tara had allowed her to contact her parents to explain everything to them.

Sonia grimaced. That had been a mess. It was all she could do to convince the senator not to send a private hostage rescue team to Liberia to escort her and his grandson back to the U.S. But that would cause an international incident, at best, and Joseph would still have the better side of the argument in any custody battle over David.

In a way, her mother's reaction had been even worse. She'd just kept crying and saying: "I knew it. I *knew* something would go wrong if you went to live in that godforsaken place." Eventually, her parents had calmed down enough to hear the plan. They weren't happy about the risk she was taking, but they understood she had few options. Still, that didn't stop them from doing all they could to help. Her father had all but threatened to hunt Tyrone and Tara down and take them out himself if anything went wrong with the operation and she or their grandson were harmed. Maybe the CIA wouldn't be so quick to deem her expendable now.

Sonia brought herself back to the present. "When do you want me to get this done?" she asked.

"That's entirely up to you. We'll keep an ear out for the triggering of the listening device and be ready to enter the mansion and make the arrest as early as tonight. Assuming all goes well, you and your son could be on the Red Cross flight to

Washington, D.C. on Wednesday morning," Tara said.

"To think that I could be free from this nightmare as early as Wednesday morning. It just seems unreal. That's assuming I don't get caught in the act and killed, of course," Sonia said.

"You're a smart, strong, and resourceful woman. I have no doubt you can get this done. Just have faith," Tara said.

"Tara will give you a bag with a hidden compartment in which to carry those supplies. If anyone looks inside the bag, they'll only find scarves and other items easily passable as gifts," Tyrone said.

"That's good. Well, we'll see how this turns out. Thank you both for everything," Sonia said.

"No. Thank you. Both Liberia and the American government will be in your debt when you pull this off and give us the evidence we need to put the Saytumah family out of business," Tara said.

It was strange. The weeks she'd spent training with Tyrone and Tara had made her feel like she was part of something larger than herself. It gave her a respite from wanting to pull her hair out in the presidential mansion. A part of her felt a little sad that the training had come to an end. *This is not the time to get irrational and emotional. You've got a mission to complete.*

She glanced at her watch and, to her surprise, saw that it was nearly dinnertime. "It's getting late. I'd better get back before Joseph gets suspicious."

"Good luck and be careful," Tara said.

"We have faith in you," Tyrone said.

Sonia took a deep breath and pushed it out. "Thank you. Let's just hope your faith in me is justified."

***

A few hours later, Tyrone and Tara reported to their handler by teleconference.

"We're ready to mobilize as soon as we get a signal from Sonia's earpiece," Tara said.

"Are you sure she'll be able to pull this off?" the handler asked.

Tyrone shrugged. "She's a resourceful woman. Her husband may believe that she'd try to smuggle their son out of the country, but she hasn't given him any reason to believe she'd help us spy on his operations. That should give her an advantage."

"Well, she's going to have to move soon," the handler said. "The Saytumah family is expected to receive a large shipment of weapons in the next few days. We need to wrap this up before then."

Tara nodded. "We understand. If Sonia doesn't activate by tomorrow, we'll visit the Presidential mansion and pass on the message."

***

The next evening, Sonia lay on the bed in the master bedroom of the Presidential mansion. Joseph and the Saytumah family doctor stood beside it.

"What is wrong with her?" Joseph asked.

"From her symptoms, I would say she has a classic migraine. She describes a very bad headache, light sensitivity, aureoles of flashing lights and a partially blocked field of vision. I prescribe rest in a darkened room and Imitrex which is a migraine medication," the doctor said.

"We have a very important function to attend at the U.S. Embassy tonight. Are you sure you cannot give her something that will enable her to go?" Joseph asked.

"No. I cannot recommend that she attend any function in her state. Her equilibrium is off, she's nauseous and in much pain. She needs to rest," the doctor said.

Most people would have bowed under the pressure of the president's glare; however, the doctor remained impassive. He had helped Joseph's mother give birth to him and had served as the Saytumah family doctor ever since.

Joseph sighed. "Very well. I will, of course, cede to your diagnosis. How does one get these classic migraines?"

"They can be triggered by a number of things, such as the consumption of chocolate, red wines, and nuts. Stress can certainly trigger them, as well as changes in hormone levels."

"Hormones? Is she pregnant?" Joseph asked.

"No, I'm not pregnant. And by the way, I'm right here. Will you two please let me be so I can rest? And please, please, turn off that light. My head is killing me," Sonia said.

"Certainly, Madame Saytumah. Take two of these pills every four hours as needed and get some rest." The doctor held a bottle of pills out to her.

"Thank you, Doctor." Sonia took the bottle from him.

While the doctor packed up his medical bag and said his goodbyes, Sonia opened the pill bottle and poured two pills into her hand. She reached for the glass of water sitting on her nightstand and pretended to take the medicine. She slipped the pills under her tongue, drank a sip of the water, threw her head back and swallowed.

The doctor nodded in approval. "Take good care of yourself, my lady."

"I will, Doctor," Sonia said.

As soon as Joseph and the doctor left the bedroom, Sonia spat the pills out into her hand, wrapped them in a tissue, and threw them into the wastepaper basket by the bed. The tissue had just landed when Joseph returned to the bedroom.

"I really needed for you to attend the function with me tonight. I am not an ogre, however. Given your condition, I will attend the function alone. You stay here and get some rest. I fully expect you to be fit enough to attend tomorrow's event at the embassy. Since you appear to be prone to getting these migraines, I will instruct the kitchen staff to limit your intake of the foods the doctor identified as triggers," he said.

"Joseph, I'm not a child. I'm fully capable of limiting my own intake of the foods the doctor identified as triggers," she said.

"We will discuss this in more detail some other time. Right now, I need to leave. The embassy function begins in an hour and the roads have not been in the greatest condition since the recent storm. I will see you later, darling." He leaned down and kissed her on her forehead. She closed her eyes and said nothing. He stared down at her for a moment, then left.

Sonia lay there in bed for a while. After ten minutes, she got up, pulled on a pair of black pants, a black top and a pair of soft loafers. She pulled her hair back into a ponytail then headed into the master closet and pulled out the bag Tara had given her. She rummaged down to the bottom of the bag, opened the false bottom and extracted the pistol, the ammunition clips, the earpiece and the disc drive device.

She pulled a black messenger bag off a shelf in the closet and put the weapon, the clips and the device inside. She pressed a button on the ear piece and placed it in her ear, then she slung the purse around her body crosswise.

"This is Sonia," she said. "Can anyone hear me?"

"We hear you loud and clear, Sonia," Tara said.

"Tonight's the night. Do you understand? My husband is away and I am going for the information tonight," Sonia said.

"Understood. Keep your communication device on. We'll be with you every step of the way. Where is Joseph?" Tara asked.

"He is at a United States Embassy function," Sonia said.

"Good. If he's at the embassy, we can keep an eye on him and inform you when he leaves," Tara said.

"Good. Thank you," Sonia said. She took a deep breath and released it. "Well, here goes nothing."

Chapter XVI

Sonia opened the door to the master bedroom and peered out. No-one was in the hallway. She slipped out, closed the door, leaned against it for a moment, and listened. The house was quiet.

She turned right and walked down the hallway to the living room. No-one else was there. The servants had probably retired to their quarters for the evening. She crossed the living room and turned down the left corridor that led to the nonresidential portion of the Presidential mansion. She passed several offices. The doors were closed. She could see no lights shining under them. No–one appeared to be working late tonight.

When the cat's away, the mice will play. She stifled a hysterical giggle.

She walked quietly up to the door of the Presidential office. She put her ear against it and listened for any sound coming from within. There was nothing but silence. She closed her eyes for a moment, said a silent prayer, and slowly turned the knob. When it had twisted all the way, she pushed opened the door. The office was dark.

She stepped in, closed the door behind her, then tiptoed past the small area where Fatima used to sit and entered the larger section where her husband worked. She felt along the wall until she located a light switch and flipped it on. The empty office looked different than it did during the hustle and bustle of the day. Somehow, it seemed more elegant. There was a sense of history in the furnishings, the books, and the artwork. She shook it off. This was no time for sightseeing.

"Get with the program," she murmured under her breath.

"Did you say something, Sonia?" Tara asked.

Sonia jumped. She didn't realize she had spoken out loud and forgot that she was wearing the earpiece. "I'm in the Presidential office."

"Good," Tara said. "Now go over to the desk and turn on the computer."

"Okay." Sonia crossed the office, went behind the desk, pulled the large chair back, crouched down, and searched for the computer's power switch. She pressed it and jumped at the sound of the computer coming to life. She took a deep breath and expelled it. "It's on."

"Good," Tara said. "Now plug the device into a USB slot."

"Okay." Sonia got down onto her knees and searched for a USB slot on the back of the computer tower. When she found one, she pulled the device from her bag, plugged it in and stood up. "Done," she said. "What now?"

"The upload is working. We're receiving the information. Just let the device do its thing," Tara said.

Sonia sat in the large leather desk chair and watched the computer screen. What appeared to be file names flew across it at almost lightning speed. After a minute or so, she began to get anxious. "How much longer?"

"I don't know," Tara said. "It depends on the amount of data in the computer."

"I can't stay in here much longer," Sonia said.

"Don't worry," Tara said, "Joseph is still at the embassy."

"Yeah, but what am I going to do if a guard or someone else comes in here?" Sonia asked.

"We went over that. Remember? You just tell them that Joseph asked you to retrieve some information for him and bluff your way out. If that doesn't work, Plan B is for us to retrieve you," Tara said.

"Right," Sonia said. She crossed the office, put her head against the door and listened. She heard the faint sound of footsteps. It sounded as if someone were slowly coming down the hallway toward the office. Her heart leapt into her throat. She flicked off the light and tiptoed quickly across the floor to a door she had noticed on the other side of the room. Squinting her eyes, trying to see in the dark, she held out her hand feeling for the far wall. When her hand hit it, she put her back against it and slid to her right, searching for the door. She stared in the dark toward the front door of the office and listened. The footsteps got louder.

"Oh my God." Sonia's voice was barely a whisper.

"What?" Tara asked.

"Someone's coming."

"Remember the game plan," Tara said.

"Too late," Sonia said. "I turned out the light and decided to hide instead."

"What?" Tara's voice was a hiss in her ear. "Why did you do that?"

"Shh," Sonia said, "I can't talk now." Her hand hit the door knob. She said a silent prayer that it would be open. She twisted the knob and pressed against the door. It opened. Breathing a sigh of relief, she slipped inside and had just pushed the door shut again when she heard the door to the office open.

Whoever entered the office turned on the lights. She could see the light in the small space under the door she'd just closed. Sonia held her breath. She prayed that whoever it was wouldn't notice the computer was on or see the file names flying across the screen. She heard the door to the office close then heard footsteps crossing the office. Soon, she heard the sounds of drawers opening and closing and the tap of computer keys.

"Oho! What have we here?"

Sonia's blood froze. It couldn't be. It sounded like Saye. Her mind raced. If it was Saye, he hadn't come here to see Joseph. He'd disappeared after David's kidnapping. Joseph told her he suspected his brother had been the brains behind the operation, because he and Fatimah were lovers. Saye had to know Joseph had issued orders for his arrest and that Joseph's men were looking for him.

"Saye," Sonia whispered.

"What? Did you say Saye? Is he there?" Tara asked.

Sonia tiptoed away from the door. "Yes," she whispered. "I think he's in the Presidential office and that he just discovered the uplink."

"Where are you?" Tara asked.

Sonia glanced around. There were file cabinets lined up against the walls and a photocopier. "I'm in some sort of file room inside the Presidential office suite."

"Hold on," Tara said. Sonia heard a muffled conversation – as if Tara had placed her hand over the receiver of a telephone. After a moment, Tara spoke. "The uplink has stopped. Saye must have pulled the device from the computer. But it looks as if we already have more than we need to prosecute."

Relief poured through Sonia. "Thank God."

"Listen to me carefully," Tara said. "We're on our way and will be at the Presidential mansion in ten minutes. Keep this link open and stay in that file room. Do not move. Do you hear me?"

"Yes," Sonia said. "I hear you. But what about my son? I have to get to him."

"No," Tara said. "He's asleep in his nursery, right? That's the safest place for him to be right now. You don't want to have him anywhere near you in the event you're discovered. This is for the best."

She thought about it. David certainly wouldn't be safe with her in the file room. And it wasn't as if she had a plan for getting to him at this point anyway. She walked over to the door of the file room again, pressed her ear up against it and listened. All she heard was silence.

"Í can't hear anything," she whispered. "Saye must have left."

"Whatever you do, don't open that door," Tara said. "If he's still in there and you open the door, you'll be exposed."

Sonia's anxiety levels rose as she waited. She had to get out of this file room. The longer she stayed there, the more likely she was to get caught. If she could just get back to the bedroom or to the nursery unseen, she'd be good to go. Joseph would blame the uplink on someone else.

She pressed her ear to the file room door and listened for another five minutes. Upon hearing nothing, she decided to take a chance. She put her hand on the knob and turned it ever so slowly until it would no longer turn. Breathing a silent prayer, she pushed the door open just a crack. The lights in the office were off.

Sonia smiled. Her risk had paid off. "They're gone,"

"What? Who's gone? Don't tell me you opened the door," Tara said.

"Yes, I did," Sonia said. "Now, I'm going to see about my son." She walked across the Presidential office and headed toward the exit.

The desk lamp clicked on. She gasped and whipped her head around to look. She saw the outline of a man sitting at the desk. Adrenaline kicked in. Her heart began to pound.

The man leaned forward. It was Saye.

"So," he said, "it is you who did this." He held up the drive.

Sonia's mind raced as she wondered how to play it. She decided to try to bluff her way out. "Saye! What are you doing here?"

"I could ask the same of you, except I know what you've been doing. I knew that whoever put this device on my brother's computer would have to come back for it. So I waited. I had no idea though that little Sonia would become a player."

"A player? What device? What are you talking about?" she asked.

"Don't play dumb with me. You are anything but dumb. Why do you think Joseph chose you? Did you think it was solely for your pretty face and firm behind? Those come a dime a dozen here in Liberia." He looked her over. "Although, you are very gifted in that sense too."

Sonia fought the urge to cross her arms over her chest. If allowing Saye to ogle her would distract him or at least keep him talking until Tara and Tyrone could get there, then let him ogle away. "What do you mean he chose me?"

"Joseph had his eye on you ever since college. My father sent him to America to get an education and to find an American-born wife with the skills, knowledge and connections to take our little operation to the next level. Like the good son he has always been, he took that charge very seriously. He was already obsessed with you. But when he learned that you planned to attend law school and that you were the daughter of a powerful U.S. Senator, it was even easier for him to sell you as a potential candidate to my father. The fact that he found you only served to prove to my father, once again, that he had chosen the right son to be his successor." Saye's tone was bitter.

Sonia swallowed hard. It was one thing to know that Joseph had used her. It was another to know that he'd been sent to America for that very purpose. "You mean . . . you mean he's been planning this ever since we were in college? But why? For God's sake, why?"

"So that when we executed the coup d'état you'd be able to help negotiate with the U.S. and other countries to give aid to Liberia and to help legitimize the new government. My father was supposed to execute the coup but he died before we could get all the pieces in place. After his death, I always thought it would be me who took the reins, but Joseph beat me to the punch. He was always doing that – taking things he had no right to. This is my birthright. I am the eldest son. I should have been my father's successor – not Joseph." He swept an arm across the desk. Pens, papers, photo frames and other items fell onto the floor. He looked up at Sonia. The rage and madness burned brightly in his eyes.

This man is out of his damned mind. What am I going to do?

She thought about the gun in her bag. She really didn't want to have to shoot her way out, but if that was her only option, she'd take it. But how would she get the gun out and the safety off fast enough to use it?

"Keep him talking, Sonia. We're five minutes away." Tara's voice was quiet in her ear.

"Wow," she said. "Here I was thinking that Joseph changed once we got to Liberia. I had no idea he'd been planning this since college." She stepped over to a small desk on the other side of the room to put some distance between them and sagged against it, as if in shock. "I was just a pawn in his little game." She shook her head.

Saye laughed. "We are all just pawns in my father and Joseph's little games. But no longer. So, Sonia, what are you doing here? Who are you? A spy for the U.S. government? Or are you just working for them? Are you having fun playing Jane Bond? I heard that Joseph was keeping you hostage here and that he wouldn't let you take my little nephew out of the country. How is little David after his terrible ordeal? Did those bad men hurt him?"

The fact that he could make light of the kidnapping and the hell he had put them through made Sonia forget all about keeping him calm and talking. She wanted to slap him. She stood up straight, put her hands on her hips and narrowed her eyes at him. "Don't you ever mention my son's name again, you son of a bitch. How could you? How could you arrange to have your own nephew kidnapped and then joke about it? He's just an innocent little boy."

"There is no such thing as innocent in Liberia. Children younger than my nephew are witness to terrible atrocities if not the subjects themselves. Joseph was kidnapped when he was just a boy and his kidnappers did not treat him so nicely. They whipped him to within an inch of his young life," Saye said.

"I know," Sonia said. "He told me about that while we were in college. They did that just to get back at your father. It's one of the reasons I'm so determined to get David somewhere safe – out of this madness."

Saye laughed. "Safe? Do you think anywhere is safe? Even if you did manage to get David out of the country, Joseph would hunt you to the ends of the Earth to get him back. And if he didn't get you, one of his enemies would. But don't worry, my dear. It will all be over soon." He sent her an evil grin.

"Over soon? What do you mean by that?"

"My men are on their way here as we speak. I am here to claim the government of Liberia. I am executing a coup d'état and you are my first prisoner. It will be nice to have you chained up in my dungeon for as long as it amuses me. As for David," he shrugged, "it is best not to leave any former heirs to the throne lingering about."

Sonia saw red. She pushed off the desk and started to take a step toward Saye fully intending to rip his throat out with her bare hands. As if she could sense Sonia's intent, Tara spoke up.

"Sonia," she said, "keep your cool. Don't blow it. We're calling in a contingent of men to intercept Saye's men before they hit the mansion. We are already outside. Now, we have to take out the guards. We've got a plan to get you and David out, but it depends on you keeping your cool. Keep him talking. Do you hear me? Keep him talking."

Saye watched Sonia, a curious expression on his face. He knew she was desperate to keep her son safe. She'd play into that -- offer him a proposition -- maybe flirt with him a little. Anything to buy time.

She took a couple of steps toward him and plastered on a smile. "I'm a woman. I know how this works. Surely we can work something out. You don't need to lock me up to get me to cooperate. You don't have to kill my son either. All I ever wanted to do was to keep him safe. Let me send him to his grandparents in the U.S. I could stay here and work for your administration as your assistant or whatever. And at night, I could be anything you need." She licked her lips suggestively.

Saye stared at her lips and seemed to consider her offer. After a moment, he sighed, then shook his head. "Although it is a pity, and a waste, I am afraid I cannot take you up on your offer. You see, you can't be trusted." He held up the electronic gadget. "Where did you get this and what were you doing with it?"

Seeking to restore the distance between them, Sonia flounced back to the small desk as if insulted. "Humph." She crossed her arms in front of her chest. "I have no idea what you're talking about."

"Don't play coy with me, you bitch." He leaned forward in his seat. "I asked you a question and I expect a prompt answer. What is this and where did you get it?"

Sonia looked him in the eye to distract him, at the same time, she eased her hand into her bag and gripped the barrel of the gun. "Look, I don't know what that is or where it came from. I was in the file room copying some files to bring to my husband. He called and asked me to do it since no-one else was here."

Saye pushed back his chair and stood up. "I see that I am going to have to teach you a lesson."

Sonia pulled the gun from her bag, thumbed off the safety and aimed it at him. "I suggest you sit your ass back down in that chair."

Saye stood there looking at her in open-mouthed astonishment.

"I said sit down," she said.

Saye sat. "How dare you pull a gun on me? As soon as my men get here and take the mansion, I will have your fingernails pulled off one at a time for that."

"How do you know you'll live to see your men take the mansion?" Sonia asked.

Saye looked at her. "You wouldn't dare shoot me." He put his hands on the desk, pushed back his chair and stood up.

Sonia backed away. "I assure you that I will shoot you if you don't sit back down."

"No you won't. If you were going to shoot me, you would have done it by now." He turned and started to come around the desk. Sonia fired off a shot. The bullet caught him in his right arm. Blood spurted out.

"Ow!" He grabbed his arm. "You fucking bitch! You shot me!" Breathing heavily, he dropped back into his seat.

"Yes, I did. If you don't stay down, I'll shoot you again. Next time, it won't be in the arm."

Chapter XVII

Outside the mansion, Tara, Tyrone and a contingent of men crept along the grounds. They'd tranquilized the guard dogs. Now, they had to neutralize the guards. Some of them walked the grounds making their appointed rounds. Two of them appeared to be on break. They played dominoes in a small room off the foyer. Tyrone peaked through the window at them. He turned to Tara and held up two fingers, indicating that she should take those two out. The others would take the guards outside. Tara nodded.

Tyrone crept to the edge of the mansion and peered around the corner. One of the guards was smoking a cigarette. Tyrone walked silently up to him and grabbed him in a chokehold from behind. He used his forearms to cut off the guard's air. The guard struggled mightily, but Tyrone held on until he felt the man slump against him. He then eased the guard down to the ground and dragged him behind some foliage. He stood there for a moment, listening, until he was satisfied no-one had seen or heard the struggle. He looked to his right and saw one of his men take out another guard. He went in search of the others.

Tara pulled her tranquilizer gun. She put her back against the wall, took a deep breath and blew it out. She then stepped through the open doorway took aim and fired two shots. Her aim was dead-on. The men went down. They never had a chance to make a sound or pull their weapons. One of the men fell out of his chair and onto the floor, overturning it in the process. The sound was deafening to Tara's ears. She froze for a moment, trying to figure out whether the noise had alerted anyone. There was silence. She pulled a device from her fanny pack and crossed the room. She then extended her arm and aimed the device in the general direction of the surveillance camera she knew would be to the left of the doorway and pressed a switch.

"I'm in," she heard Naimah say into her earpiece.

She switched her com over to check on Sonia. That's when she heard the muffled sound of a silenced gunshot. Her heart leapt into her throat. *Please God, please let Sonia be okay.*

"Sonia. Sonia, are you alright?"

"Yes. I'm fine," Sonia said. "Saye's not though. I just shot him in the arm."

Tara sighed, her eyes fluttering closed for a second. "We've neutralized the outside guards and are on our way inside. Just hold on a little longer. Hold on."

Tara heard Naimah's voice in her other ear. "Tara, President Saytumahs' limousine has been spotted on the road. Repeat, President Saytumah is en route to the Presidential mansion.

Tara cursed. They were supposed to be notified when Joseph left the American embassy -- not when he and his contingent of bodyguards were already en route. If they made it out of this op alive, heads were going roll. Now, however, was not the time for recriminations. "ETA?" she asked.

"Ten minutes," Naimah said.

"Oh no," Tara said.

"Oh no? What? Don't say that. What's going on?" Sonia asked.

"Joseph somehow eluded our watchers. We just received a report that his limousine is headed this way. Some of us are going to hide. Hopefully, he won't notice that the guards patrolling the grounds are imposters. We're going to have to take the mansion with him inside. Sorry Sonia, it's best that way."

"Sorry? Best way for who? Are you insane? What am I supposed to tell Joseph when he gets here and finds me and Saye in his office and Saye shot?" Sonia asked.

"You'll have to improvise," Tara said.

***

Improvise? Sonia felt a mixture of panic and anger rise up inside of her. If she lived through this night, she'd have a few things to say to the CIA. But she'd have to survive first.

She glanced over at Saye. He was sitting there, holding his arm and watching her, an amused expression on his face.

"So," he said, "my brother did not send you in here after all. How will you explain your presence here, Sonia? And how will you explain this?" He held out the electronic gadget he had pulled from the computer. "My brother will kill you when he finds out you have betrayed him. That will save me the trouble."

"Shut up," Sonia said. She paced back and forth, trying to think. "He's certainly going to kill you when he finds out what you came here to do. He'll thank me for shooting you. I'll just tell him that I heard noises while walking past, came in here to investigate, and then caught you in here."

But how would she explain the gun? She continued to pace, filled with dread for Joseph's arrival. She caught a movement in the corner of her eye and whipped her head around just in time to see Saye aiming a gun at her. She turned and dove behind the secretarial desk as a shot rang out. Her heart beat wildly as she crouched behind it trying to figure out what to do. She cursed. Where the hell had he gotten that gun and why didn't she think to search him when she had the chance?

It was becoming painfully clear to her that this was not a game. They were playing for keeps and, if Saye had his way, her son would be killed. She had to protect him and she had to stay alive long enough to do it.

"What happened? I heard a shot," Tara said.

"Saye has a gun," Sonia said.

"Oh no. Okay, remember your training. You've only fired one shot so far. You still have several bullets left in that clip. Stop talking to me and figure out what you have to do. Where is he now?"

Sonia listened but all she heard was silence. She crawled over to one side of the desk and peeked around the corner. Saye was still sitting behind the larger desk. When she poked her head out, he aimed the gun at her and fired again. She pulled back just in time. The bullet hit the side of the desk where her head had been. Wood chips flew everywhere. Sonia cried out.

Saye slid his chair back, stood up, and began to advance in Sonia's direction. "You won't get out of here alive, Sonia," That may be a blessing in disguise for you. I had so many plans in store for you. I doubt you would have enjoyed them as much as I would have. Now, we'll never know."

Sonia crouched, her heart thudding against her ribs, pondering her next move. She knew she couldn't just sit there like a doe in the headlights. He'd shoot her as soon as he got her in his sights. She had to move if she wanted to stay alive. But how? As much as she liked action movies, none of the scenes she'd watched seemed plausible in real life. This was not the movies.

She decided to do the only thing she knew how to do -- confront him directly. She only hoped the element of surprise would allow her to get a shot off first. She stood up quickly, aimed and fired off a shot. Saye's eyes widened for a second, then he fired. Thankfully, he missed. Her shot must have thrown his aim off. He fell backward onto the floor, clutching at his chest. The gun fell from his hand and clattered onto the floor next to him.

"You shot me again, you bitch!" His voice was strained with pain and his breathing was labored.

"You left me no choice," Sonia said. "It was you or me and my son needs me." She kept her gun aimed at him and took a step in his direction. She'd intended to kick the gun away from him and search him for other weapons. At that moment, however, the door to the office flew open. Joseph's personal guard stepped in with Joseph following closely behind, their weapons drawn. The guard, upon seeing Saye on the floor, immediately aimed his gun at him.

Joseph looked from his wife to his brother and lowered his weapon. "What is going on here?" He stepped toward Sonia.

Sonia flinched and took a step backward. Joseph stared at her for a moment then walked over to his brother. Saye lay bleeding on the floor, looking up at Joseph with hate-filled eyes.

He laughed. It was not a mirthful sound. "As usual, you have no idea what is going on, little brother."

"What are you doing here, Saye? I have been looking for you and that worthless whore Fatima. I know you both were involved in my son's kidnapping. You have a lot of balls coming here tonight, brother. Too bad they won't be a part of your body much longer."

"I am here to take over the Presidency of Liberia. My men will be here soon. There is nothing you can do to stop me," Saye said.

"It looks as if my wife already has," Joseph said. "I bet you never expected to have your master plan thwarted by a woman." He threw back his head and laughed.

Saye's face filled with rage. "You fucking bastard! How dare you laugh at me? This is my birthright – not yours! I am the eldest son and the heir to the throne – not you!   None of this would have happened but for your greedy, power-hungry ass. You had to have it all, didn't you -- control of father's company, control of the country. What gave you the right to have it all?"

"Who gave you the right to kidnap my son? Your own nephew? Father would turn over in his grave if he saw the poor excuse of a man you have become. We both made our choices a long time ago. You chose to party, have a good time, and never take responsibility for your own actions. I chose to follow in father's footsteps. This is where it led us. It turned you into a traitor – to your country and your family, and me into the president of Liberia" Joseph said.

"It turned you into a megalomaniac who doesn't even have control over his own house," Saye said.

"What are you talking about?" Joseph asked.

"I'm talking about the device on top of your desk," Saye said. A triumphant smile came over Saye's face. "It is a special drive designed to download all of the information contained in your computer and send it to the American government. I found it plugged into the computer when I got here. I also found your lovely wife hiding in the file room."

Sonia saw Joseph's eyebrows furrow together. He walked over to the desk, picked up the gadget with his left hand and looked it over. Then he looked at Sonia. "What is this?"

Sonia's mind raced as she tried to figure out what to say.

"We are in the mansion heading toward the office," Tara said in her ear. "Stall them for as long as you can."

"I don't know what that is," Sonia said, "and I have no idea what he's talking about. After my headache passed, I was restless. So, I came in here to get some paper to work on ideas for my book. I went into the file room looking for a legal pad or something. When I came out, Saye was there sitting at your desk. He said he was going to kill you and David, take over the country, and chain me up in the basement so that he could play with me."

"Where did you get that gun?" Joseph asked.

"I . . . it was on the desk here. I noticed it when I came out of the file room. While he was talking to me, I backed up until I got to the desk, then I grabbed the gun and threw myself behind it. Thank

God somebody left it there. I was lucky enough to get the drop on him. Oh Joseph, I was so scared."

Joseph looked at the device in his hand, then he looked at his brother.

Sonia took a step toward Joseph, thinking she would continue the charade by throwing herself into his arms. At that moment, however, he turned to look at her, and the hurt and betrayal she saw in his eyes stopped her in her tracks.

"You are lying to me," he said. "We will deal with that later. First, I need to deal with my brother." He turned toward Saye. "Goodbye, brother. May you live a better life and be a better person the next time you walk this Earth." He aimed his weapon and pulled the trigger. A bullet hole erupted right between Saye's eyes.

Sonia stared at Saye's limp body and wondered whether she would be next. She aimed her gun at Joseph.

He aimed his gun at her. "Who are you working for?"

Sonia blinked. She had half expected for him to simply turn and pull the trigger. "What?"

"Who are you working for? Are you working for the American government? Are you a spy? Do you work for one of my political enemies in Liberia? Who?"

"I don't know what you mean," she said.

"Stop lying to me." He held up the electronic device. "Saye had just as much to lose as I did if the information in my computer was downloaded by someone else. If the Americans got it, he would be subject to prosecution. If our enemies got it, they could use it to run us out of power and out of business. My brother was many things, but he was not stupid, and I could always rely upon him to be greedy and to act in his own self-interest. That's how I knew he was telling the truth when he told me you had betrayed me and showed me this. So I ask you, for the last time, who are you working for?"

Sonia swallowed. "I'm not working for anyone. All I ever wanted was for David to be safe. The American government demanded that I secure information from your computer in exchange for giving us safe passage to America. I never wanted to betray you. I begged you to let us go."

Joseph shook his head. "How could you do this to me? To us?"

She thought about trying to placate him but knew it would be useless. He fully intended to kill her. She was tired of holding her tongue. If she was going to die, then she would go out saying what needed to be said. "News flash, Joseph. It's not all about you and what you want. There are much more important things on this Earth than your goals, dreams and ambitions, such as the safety of your son. And as for us – there is no us. Any us there was died when I learned you had planned this all along and then forced me and David to stay here in Liberia after the coup. You killed us – not me," she said. "If there ever was an us." Tears streamed down her face. She dashed them away. Now was not the time to cry.

She watched a series of emotions cross her husband's face. When she saw resignation and resolve come into his eyes, she knew she had to take him out or he would kill her. She raised her gun and fired. She hit her target, but that didn't stop him from pulling the trigger.

Sonia felt a searing pain hit her in the chest before she heard the shot. The bullet knocked her backward off her feet and onto the floor. While she lay there, she dimly heard the sound of the office door crashing in. Her last thought was of her son. He would now grow up without his parents, but at least he'd be safe with hers in America. Sonia smiled at that thought, then the world grew dark as she lost consciousness.

***

Tara, Tyrone and a contingent of U.S. soldiers entered the Presidential office. Tara surveyed the scene and saw Sonia, Joseph and Saye lying on the floor. She ran over to Sonia and placed two fingers against her neck. She felt a faint pulse. "She's alive. Get a medic in here."

Tara caught a motion in the corner of her eye and turned to look. Joseph, who was apparently wounded, but not dead, brought his weapon up and aimed it at Sonia. Tara cursed. She dropped to the floor to shield Sonia, intending to protect her with her Kevlar vest. Joseph fired. The bullet hit Tara's shoulder.

Tyrone pumped a round between Joseph's eyes and two more in his chest. He then ran over to check on Tara. The wound hurt like a bitch. She writhed in agony and cursed up a blue streak.

"Tara! Where are you hit?" Tyrone tried to hold her still so he could see for himself.

Tara clenched her teeth against the pain. "My shoulder."

"Medic! We need two gurneys!" Tyrone opened his emergency kit, extracted a bandage, pressed it against Tara's shoulder and applied pressure to stop the bleeding.

Tara struggled to sit up but Tyrone held her down. They had to help Sonia. She'd be damned if she'd lose another casualty to that son of a bitch Joseph.

"No. Don't get up, sis. Just take it easy," Tyrone said.

"But Sonia," Tara said.

"The medic is taking care of her now," he said. "You're next. Just hold on."

Chapter XVIII

Sonia opened her eyes and wondered if she had died and gone to heaven. Everything was white. She blinked trying to adjust to the almost blinding light. After a few moments, she realized that she was lying in a bed looking up at a white ceiling. Slowly, she became aware of the IV drip in her right arm and the bandages covering her chest.

She heard a low buzzing sound to her left and turned her head to find the source. Her mother was fast asleep in a chair next to the bed, snoring. She studied her for a moment and wondered whether to wake her. The poor woman looked exhausted. Her usually perfectly coiffed hair was a little disheveled. Tendrils had started to fall from the bun on top of her head and coil around her cheeks. She wasn't wearing any makeup either. Lines that Sonia had never noticed before had started to form around her mouth. Guilt swamped Sonia at the thought that she was responsible for putting them there. Her parents must have been worried sick. Now that she was a mother herself, she understood that primal and overwhelming need to protect one's child.

David! Where was he? She had to know. She tried to say something -- to call out to her mother, but it came out more like a mumble. Her mouth was so dry. She swallowed, cleared her throat, and tried again.

"Mom," she said.

Her mother opened her eyes, stretched a little, and looked at Sonia. Her eyes widened then she jumped up out of the chair and rushed to her bedside. "Sonia? Oh baby, you're awake." She raised her eyes to the ceiling. "Thank God. Thank you, Lord." She hugged Sonia and planted kisses all over her face.

Sonia smiled and started to laugh, but it hurt too much. She groaned.

Her mother frowned. "How do you feel? Are you in pain? Let me get the doctor."

Before Sonia could say a word, her mother rushed out of the room shouting for the nurse. "She's awake! My daughter is awake! Get the doctor." Mrs. Johnson returned to Sonia's bedside.

Sonia grabbed her arm to get her attention. "David?"

Her mom patted her hand. "He's fine, sweetie. He's at home with your father."

Sonia closed her eyes in relief. David was safe. Thank God. Now if she could just keep him that way. The only way to do that was to make sure Joseph couldn't take him back to Liberia. She opened her eyes. "Joseph?"

Her mother shook her head and squeezed her hand. "I can't imagine what you must have gone through, dear. I almost died a thousand deaths when they told me what happened and that you were in the hospital." Tears filled her eyes. "We thought we were going to lose you."

"Oh mom, I'm so sorry. I never wanted to put you through that. I didn't know. I didn't know until it was too late," she said. They cried together for a moment.

Her mother straightened when the doctor and the nurse walked into the room. She grabbed some tissues from the bedside table and wiped her face. "Enough. You're back, alive, and safe. I have to call your father and let him know."

"You're a very lucky woman," the doctor said. He checked her pulse.

"You have no idea," Sonia said.

"I think I have a clue. The bullet did extensive internal damage. You went into a coma and we weren't sure when or if you'd come out," he said.

"How long have I been out?" Sonia asked.

"It's been two weeks," he said.

After the doctor and nurses left, Sonia's mother came back into the room. "There's someone here to see you," she said. She stepped aside.

Tara stood behind her. She was hooked up to a portable IV stand.

Sonia smiled. "Tara! Oh thank God. I thought I'd never see you again. Come here, girl!"

Tara grinned and walked over to the bed. "It's good to see you too. You've been unconscious for a while now. We weren't sure you'd pull through. But I should have known you would, being stubborn as hell. I was tempted to kill you myself when you decided to leave that file room after I specifically told you not to."

"I was going crazy in that place. I had to get to my son," Sonia said.

Tara nodded. "I understand."

"So, what happened?" Sonia asked. "The last thing I remember was shooting Joseph and him shooting me. Is he still alive?"

"No. You hit him, but you missed his heart. He was still alive when we got there. When he heard you were still alive, he tried to shoot you again. I blocked the shot hoping he would hit the vest, but he got me in the shoulder. That's when Tyrone took his ass out. Sorry ma'am," Tara said, glancing at Mrs. Johnson.

Sonia's mother shook her head. "You jumped in front of a bullet meant for my daughter. You can say any damned thing you want. There's no need to apologize. We owe you a debt we can never repay."

"Yes. Thank you Tara. You saved my life," Sonia said. "What about Saye?"

"We found him lying on the ground. He was dead," Tara said.

With both Joseph and Saye dead, who will take over Liberia?" Sonia asked.

"President Sirleaf has been reinstated as the president of Liberia," Tara said.

That was as it should be. Sonia nodded. "Good. Since both Joseph and Saye are dead, there's no need for us to go into the witness protection program, right?"

"Well, it is less likely that anyone will come after you and David; however, we still recommend you go into the program. There is still an outside chance that persons loyal to them will seek revenge," Tara said.

Sonia thought about it for a moment. "No. David and I aren't going to live the rest of our lives in hiding. What happened in Liberia is in the past. We've got to look toward the future now."

"But Sonia," Tara said, "Joseph and Saye had cousins. You met some of them at Dwe's birthday party. While we have no evidence they were ever involved in Dwe's business or in politics, you never know what they'll do when they learn that Joseph and Saye are dead. We've done everything possible to keep how they died a secret, but you know how it is. There were guards and servants in the mansion. Once they tell others what they observed, people will piece it together. You really should consider going into the program."

Sonia sighed and closed her eyes. "I'll consider it, Tara, but I don't believe I'll change my mind."

Tara put her hand over Sonia's. "That's all I can ask. Get some rest." She left the room.

A half hour later, the door to Sonia's room opened again. It was her father and David. Before his

222 L.J. TAYLOR

grandfather could stop him, David ran up to his mother's bed, climbed up on it and gave her a kiss.

Sonia smiled, hugged her son tightly and kissed his little cheeks, oblivious to the pain caused by his weight laying across her bandages. "Baby, I'm so happy to see you." She smiled up at her father and held out one of her hands to him.

He took it and squeezed. "Welcome back, love."

Sonia blinked back tears and rubbed her face against her son's smooth cheek. She and her son were safe and back in the States. Life didn't get much better than this.

***

Later that evening, after visiting hours were over, Sonia slept peacefully in her hospital bed. She dreamed she was on a beach building sandcastles with David. Sea gulls flew around them. There wasn't a cloud in the sky.

Suddenly, the sky darkened. Wind whipped the sand up with a fury and sent waves crashing onto the beach. The tide rose and the waves got bigger and bigger. A large tidal wave formed and headed toward the beach. She scooped David up and began running toward the parking lot. She struggled to breathe. The wave overtook them. She couldn't breathe. The pain was excruciating. She struggled furiously to claw her way free and get some air.

Sonia woke up to find a pillow being pressed over face and a heavy weight across her chest.

Adrenaline kicked in. She heard the pace of the beeps on her heart monitor increase. She struggled to get the pillow off her face and pushed at the heavy weight on her chest, but neither would budge. She was too weak from her injuries. Despair kicked in as she felt herself begin to lose consciousness. She couldn't die in this hospital bed -- not after she'd fought so hard to get David to safety.

In a moment of clarity, she remembered a move from Tyrone's self-defense training. She was too weak to win this fight with brute force, but if she could just get her attacker to back off, then maybe she could get some air and scream for help. She stopped struggling and let go of the pillow. She then reached up and felt for her attacker's face. Her hands came into contact with rows of braids. She grabbed the braids and yanked as hard as she could.

She heard a yelp and the pillow slid off her face. She gulped in air and raked her nails over her attacker's face. She then struck upwards with the heel of her hand under her attacker's nose as hard as she could. She heard a scream and a crashing sound.

She sat up, gasping for air, and saw Fatima sitting on the floor with her hands over her face. Blood flowed between her fingers.

"You bitch!" she screamed. "You broke my nose!"

The nurse came running into the room. "What's going on here?" she asked. "I heard a crash." She looked at Fatima. "Who are you? What are you doing in here?"

"She tried to kill me," Sonia said. She picked up the handset to the telephone next to her bed and dialed zero for the operator. "This is Sonia Saytumah. I'm in room 420. Please send security to my room right away and call the police. Someone just tried to kill me."

She heard a low metallic click and turned just in time to see Fatima grab the nurse by the arm and stab her in the chest.

"Oh my God, she has a knife! She just stabbed the nurse!" Sonia screamed.

She dropped the telephone handset and looked around for something to defend herself with. But there was nothing – only a vase of flowers her parents had brought to her room earlier and a drawing her son had left her.

Fatima let go of the nurse. She slumped to the floor. Fatima then looked up at Sonia. She looked a sight. Her nose was crooked and swollen, and her face had begun to bruise. Her lips curled back with hatred. "You're next, bitch. You took everything from me. It's time I took everything from you."

Since she had no weapon with which to defend herself, Sonia knew she had to stall Fatima until security could get to the room. "Fatima, what are you doing here? Why are you trying to kill me? What do you mean I took everything from you?"

"I waited my entire life to be the first lady. I worked for Dwe all those years so I could get close to him and his sons. But Dwe saw me like a daughter and Joseph wanted no part of me. He only had eyes for you. I was able to get close to Saye and get him to trust me, but you had to kill him. It was never enough for you to be the first lady. No. Spoiled little Sonia had to have her way and get into bed with American spies. Because of you Saye is dead and I will never get the chance to be the first lady. But you get to come here and live in America and be free. Why should you be alive and happy if Saye is dead?"

"I didn't kill Saye, Joseph did because you and he kidnapped our son. Look Fatima, I never asked for any of this. I never wanted to be involved in that saga in the first place. As far as I'm concerned, you could have had Joseph. I never wanted to be the first lady. All I ever wanted was for my son to be safe. Don't make him an orphan by killing me. Please," Sonia said.

Fatima shook her head. "It's too late." She began walking toward the bed.

The door to the room crashed in and Tara appeared in the doorway holding a gun. "Drop that knife and get away from her."

Fatima froze, momentarily. "No!" she screamed. She turned back to Sonia, raised the knife over her head and ran the last few steps to the bed.

Sonia looked up into Fatima's crazed eyes and saw her own death. She cringed.

Tara took the shot. The bullet slammed into Fatima and knocked her into the IV which crashed to the floor.

Sonia slumped back on the bed, her breathing shallow.

Medical staff and security guards raced into the room. One doctor checked the nurse and began treating her wounds. Sonia's doctor examined her to make sure she was alright. He then examined Fatima and shook his head. "She's dead."

Tara, who had been giving her report to the police, walked up to Sonia. "Are you okay?"

"I'm fine," Sonia said, "thanks to you and the self-defense training Tyrone gave me." She shook her head. "Who knew I'd need to use it while lying in a hospital bed?"

"The police want to ask you some questions. Should I make them come back tomorrow or are you up to it?" Tara asked.

"I'm up to it," Sonia said.

"After this, will you please, please let me put you and your family into the witness protection program?" Tara asked.

Sonia nodded. "Okay. You talked me into it. I have to talk to my parents about it though."

Tara nodded. "I understand. In the meantime, we're putting round the clock protection on you and your family. We don't know how many other maniacs are out there blaming you for Saye and Joseph's deaths."

"Thank you," Sonia said, "for everything. Now go and get some rest before you fall out. You're not exactly in tip top shape yourself."

Tara laughed. "No, I'm not. I think I ripped one of my stitches getting here after I got the call from security. My shoulder hurts like a bitch."

"Doctor!" Sonia called out.

Her doctor walked back into the room. "Yes?"

"Please take this maniac back to her room and check her out. She has a super hero complex and probably aggravated her injuries by racing to my rescue," Sonia said.

Tara rolled her eyes. "Now who's acting like Florence Nightingale? I'm fine."

Sonia merely raised her eyebrows and looked at her doctor.

"Come along, young lady." He took Tara by the arm and led her out of the room. "We need to take a look at those bandages. It would not surprise me if you busted a few stitches running around like that."

Sonia could hear Tara protesting all the way down the hall. She smiled.

Epilogue

A few years later, Sonia sat in the dining room of her home in a Virginia suburb grading papers. She had agreed to go into the witness protection program. They made her an English professor at Georgetown University. Her education and her writing background made her well suited for the position. The head of the English Department had his eye on her and told her during her last review that she was on track for a tenured position.

She looked out the window and watched David play with one of the neighbor's kids in her backyard. They were running around, whooping it up and spraying each other with water guns.

She smiled. David had adjusted wonderfully to his new surroundings. He had made friends and hardly asked about his father anymore. She'd tried to explain to him that his father was dead, but such things were difficult to explain to a five year old. She knew that one day she'd have to tell him the whole truth. She could only hope he wouldn't hate her for it and that he'd understand she'd done what she had to do to protect him.

She heard a knock at the front door and then the sound of her screen door opening. Tensing, she reached into her purse and grabbed the gun resting in there. She relaxed when she saw that it was just her father. She sighed and eased the weapon back into her purse. Her parents had gone into the witness protection program with her and David. She'd thought it was a lot to ask them to leave behind her father's position and all their friends, but they'd insisted. They hadn't wanted to be apart from her and David.

"Dad, you scared me. Do you know how close you came to getting shot?" She rose from the couch to give him a hug and a kiss. They sat together at the dining room table.

"If you're so scared, then maybe you should keep your door locked," he said.

He had her there. "I can't argue with that," she said.

"What? My daughter the lawyer chose not to argue about something? I never thought I'd see the day." He placed his hand over his heart playfully.

Sonia laughed. "You forget I'm not a lawyer any more – just a very proper English professor."

Her father shook his head. "No, I didn't forget anything. You'll be a lawyer until the day you die. Your license might expire, but you will always be a lawyer right down to the bone." He smiled at her.

Sonia chuckled. "Thank you. I'll take that as a compliment even though I'm not entirely sure you meant it as one." She looked out the window to check on her son and sighed.

"Dad -- do you and Mom ever regret entering into the program?" she asked.

"Of course not, baby," her father said. He reached out to take her hand. "We get to see more of you and David now than we ever did before. That means more to us than you could ever know – especially after we almost lost you both."

"I think I have a clue," she said.

They both turned to watch David and the neighbor's kid racing around the back yard. The kids looked as happy as could be and, for the moment, all was right with the world.

Book Reviews

I hope that you enjoyed my work. Book reviews are very important for purposes of spreading the word about a good story. Please leave an honest review of this story here.

GET A FREE BOOK

Sign up for the no spam newsletter at http://bit.ly/1Yzvagi and get a free copy of one of my books, exclusive material not available anywhere else, and first dibs on any promotions, appearances and prize giveaways.

Other Books by L.J. Taylor

<u>Just Dreams</u>

Love is a dirty word and passion has no place in the world of high-profile litigation.

Sparks fly when attorney Kathy Brooks agrees to represent novelist Charles Morgan, Jr. in a high-profile suit against a powerful government defense contractor. But when Charles' hidden agenda threatens to expose the government's dirty little secrets, what started out as the case of a lifetime could cost Kathy her heart, her career and even her life.

Charles doesn't just want to win the lawsuit. He wants to destroy the company responsible for his wife's death. His enemies, however, will stop at nothing to make the case go away – and that includes blackmail, kidnapping, and murder.

As the body count rises and the stakes get higher, Charles and Kathy will have to decide just how much they're willing to sacrifice for the win. To get justice, they'll have to put it all out on the line -- including each other -- and it still might not be enough.

Dreams Deferred

Liking the bad boys can get you killed. Has Ivy made that mistake again?

Ivy Brooks was always attracted to the bad boys until one day, she met the worst of them all and landed in prison as a result. Now, three years later, more mature and the mother of a beautiful little boy, she's determined to make a better life for herself and her son. She's also determined to make better choices when it comes to men and she's not sure her former cellmate's drop dead gorgeous brother Luke – a former bad boy who professes to have turned over a new leaf – is the right choice.

Just when she believes she's made a fresh start, her son's father, Zeke, finds out about him and sues for full custody. She kept her mouth shut when the police found jewelry from the heist committed by Zeke in her apartment. But now, to save her son from a life of misery, Ivy has no choice but to testify against Zeke. Luke is determined to protect Ivy and her son at any cost. Will she stay alive long enough to testify? And can she trust Luke to stand by her side without being drawn back into a life of violence?

About the Author

The oldest of six children, I grew up in New York City. As a child, I escaped my noisy siblings by voraciously reading every book in my parents' collection and every romance novel I could check out of the public library. My tastes later expanded to include classics, spy novels, and thrillers. Inspired by the stories I read, I began writing poetry and song lyrics and even tried to write a fantasy novel at the tender age of 13. I began writing novels as an adult during National November Writing Month in 2007 and have been chugging along ever since. When I'm not writing, I practice law in Miami, Florida.

Book reviews are very important for purposes of spreading the word about a good story. Please leave an honest review of this story on the site where you purchased it.

Keep up with me at:

www.ljtaylorbooks.com

https://twitter.com/@ljtaylor99

https://www.facebook.com/LJTaylorbooks

https://www.linkedin.com/in/LJTaylorbooks

https://plus.google.com/+ljtaylor99

Dedication

This book is dedicated to my father who supports me in everything that I do. I love you, Dad.

Acknowledgments

I'm going to keep this short and sweet and general for fear of leaving anyone out. First, I want to thank God for giving me the opportunity, the skills and the perseverance necessary to write this book. Next, I want to thank my friends and family for believing in and supporting me throughout this process.

I want to extend a special thanks to my accountability buddy Dr. Angela Massey who kept me on track and on the straight and narrow.

I want to thank my outside editor for helping me to whip it into shape for publication.

Finally, I want to thank my good friend Joseph B.K. Camara for inspiring me to write this story.

Copyright

The Liberian Agenda
Waterview Publishing, LLC
ISBN-13:978-1-941778-10-4

©2016 by L.J. Taylor

This book is a work of fiction. The names, characters, dialogue, incidents, and places, except for incidental references to public figures, products or services, are the product of the author's imagination and are not to be construed as real. No character in this book is based on an actual person. Any resemblance to actual events, locales or persons living or dead is entirely coincidental and unintentional. The author and publisher have made every effort to ensure the accuracy and completeness of the information contained in this book and assume no responsibility for any errors, inaccuracies, omissions, or inconsistencies contained herein.

For information about special discounts for bulk purchases, please contact the author or Waterview Publishing, LLC.

Waterview Publishing, LLC
P.O. Box 398244
Miami Beach, FL 33239
www.ljtaylorbooks.com
Printed in the U.S.A.